Human Rights

S.L. Armstrong

Storm Moon Press
Exceptional authors. Exceptional stories.

Storm Moon Press LLC
11502 Addison Chase Drive
Riverview, FL 33579

Cover art by Nathie Block

ISBN 13: 978-1-62757-111-1
ISBN 10:   1-627571-11-6

Chapter One

I'd had three masters in my life, and still, here I was, in the pound. I was nothing but a mutt, after all, and when one of the purebreeds they'd wanted so badly came up for sale, I was on the way out. Wouldn't want to risk having the pedigree of an expensive, beautiful bitch ruined by a mutt's seed. It didn't matter that Puan had adopted me when I was but four years old and trained me herself. I was her favorite stud until she'd landed one of the red-coated females that came from the High Breeders. Within two days, I was fifteen and foisted off on one of Puan's friends.

But Lienx wasn't as nice as Puan, and he didn't like the manners Puan had instilled in me. I wasn't allowed on the furniture. I wasn't to eat in the kitchen. I spent nights leashed to a small house outside in the yard. Lienx ruled his home with an iron fist, and when I misbehaved, I was thoroughly beaten. I learned quickly to remain invisible in Lienx's home, but then Lienx married, and his new wife, Moha, didn't like mutts. Within two weeks, Lienx had procured a purebreed. I was sent to the pound.

By the heavens, the pound. Cages. Left to wallow in our own filth because those in charge didn't want to bother. The food was tasteless. Sunlight was a treat once a week when we were taken out into the yards. Run. Play. Soak up the light until we were herded back into the large, hot buildings and locked away to be forgotten. Most pets came to the pound to die, and, at twenty-four, I resigned myself to such a fate. Two masters and well into my life, I wasn't the sort of pet a lovely master came looking for. Imagine my surprise when Kica came running through the pound, eager to find her newest pet.

Kica. Nine-years-old and the sweetest little girl. I think I loved her. She would play with me out in the yard, toss balls for me to run after, and she'd bring me scraps of her own meals. Little girls, though, grow up. For her sixteenth birthday, her father gifted her with a squealing, writhing purebreed with gorgeous, clear blue eyes. I saw her love for me die as the bawling mass in her arms demanded her attention. My heart broke when her father carted me back to the pound with not even a farewell kiss from Kica.

Thirty-one-years-old and back at the pound. I hated it. There was nothing I could do about it. I was nothing but a mutt, passed around. I would die here. I knew it in my very bones. There were younger, more beautiful pets to be found in the small cages, with bright eyes and unusual hair. I was plain. Forgettable. I was also tired. I didn't want to go home with someone else who would either abuse me or earn my trust and love only to betray me when something better, more expensive came along.

If I wore a collar and leash, I wanted it to *mean* something. I wanted to be *wanted*, needed. Heavens, perhaps even cherished, loved. Loved. I thought Kica had loved me. She'd said as much so many times as she'd brushed my hair, oiled my skin. But love, it seemed, was fickle. I was expected to give mine without pause, but my masters? They were allowed to gift it and take it back without any thought to my heart. Best to die in this sweltering hellhole of a building, thirsty and hungry and craving the sunlight, than to slowly wither as I bounced from home to home.

"What's down this hall?"

I couldn't help but lift my head as the question filtered down the dingy hallway. Was someone actually looking for an older pet? Surely not. Even if they were, I refused to allow my hopes to rise. There were two dozen other pets in this hall, all over the age of twenty-five and as tired as I was, that this person could potentially choose.

"Those are the older pets. Male. Ones that have been here more than once. You don't want any of them. They'll be taken care of when they've been here six months."

I hated *that* voice. Miab. He was an asshole. He liked to use the older female pets for copulation, which was—technically—against the law. Even pets knew that. We could be beaten, starved, denied water or baths, but we weren't supposed to be used sexually. Not that we weren't, but who believed a mongrel over an upstanding citizen? Miab, though, was a sick sonovabitch. He liked to hurt the females that he fucked, and none of us trusted him. I often wished to claw his eyes out.

"I want to see them. Age doesn't matter. None of your younger pets caught my attention. Maybe I need an older one."

Miab sighed, loud and annoyed. "All right. Come on."

Footsteps. None of us looked up. None of us moved. I don't think any of us wanted to go to another home. Six months, and then we'd be destroyed. Better than this indefinite hoping, and we wouldn't be a drain on the state's resources anymore.

"How old is the oldest here?" That voice was smooth, deep, and it made something in my gut flutter. "How old is the youngest?"

"Eldest is there, Henri. Has had six homes. Likes to bite. He's forty-six." Miab walked past my cage and pointed to an end cage. "Youngest is Fredrick. He's twenty-seven. Had three homes. Last home surrendered him because he attempted to seduce their youngest daughter."

The visitor walked up and down the corridor, pausing at each cage, but I didn't hear anyone move. When his shadow fell over me, I didn't bother to look up. The shadow didn't move, though, and after a moment, the visitor spoke.

"I'd like to see this one is the playroom, please. I'd also like to read his file."

Miab scoffed. "Ewan? He's had three previous homes."

"Why was he brought here?"

"The file says..." Miab flipped through paperwork, but I still didn't look up. "He was the pet to Master Dierr's daughter, but he secured her a purebreed. Ewan was no longer needed."

The visitor was quiet for a moment. "Is he sterile?"

Miab shook his head. "Not this one. We would have done it this time, but he's thirty-one. Low on the physician's priority list. If you purchase him, we can have him sterilized for you."

"No, that won't be necessary. If he proves to be headstrong, I will have my own physician perform the surgery." The visitor's shadow gestured. "Playroom, please."

The visitor walked off and Miab opened my cage door. I didn't have to look up to know he was sneering at me with disgust. His whiskers and nose would be twitching with his ears partially back. Miab's nose always twitched when he was annoyed. I sometimes thought—if the world were different and pets held the same rights as our masters—I'd laugh at him. I valued my skin, though. I didn't want a lashing. Miab reached in and clipped a leash to my collar and gave a jerk.

"Up, Ewan. Try not to piss on Sir Jiat's feet, hmm?"

I stood up and followed Miab without a moment's hesitation. Sir? That made this potential master one of The Guard. One of The Guard wanted an old mutt? I'd been owned only by citizens. Wealthy citizens, to be sure, but they held no titles, no real power in the world. One of The Guard would surely have enough wealth to buy the best purebreed, the finest the High Breeders had to offer. Why patronize a common pound? The only thing more shocking would have been a noble appearing in the corridor.

Miab shoved me into the room, my feet catching on the step that led from the hall to the playroom. I fell forward with a cry, hands flailing out to catch myself, but strong arms caught me before I smashed into the unforgiving tile floor. I shouldn't have looked up, shouldn't have met Sir Jiat's gaze, but I did. I clung to him and stared into his beautiful honey-colored eyes. Oh, many of the Feline masters had those amber eyes, but I'd never seen one that had copper at the heart of their eyes, hugging the black pupils.

His coloring was so striking I was unable to look away. I'd never seen one of his kind with such pale fur. He was one of the Jaguars. One couldn't ever mistake their ears, their muzzles, their spots. But Sir Jiat, he was practically white! His markings were barely visible. Under my hands, the fur was soft and well-kept, almost downy. He blinked slowly, his ears twitching as he helped me stand on my feet once more, and still I couldn't look away. He stood another good foot taller than me, broader, and his tail swished slowly behind him. I would have kept staring if Miab hadn't stepped in and let his cane crack across my thighs.

The pain was high and sharp and brought tears to my eyes. I fell to my knees before Sir Jiat and bowed my head, my sinuses stinging as I fought not to weep and beg for forgiveness. I hadn't been given leave to look, let alone speak, and one blow of the cane was all I thought I could endure today. Sir Jiat's image, though, was burned into my mind. Exotic and noble and strong. I wanted to go home with him. If any pet could instantly want to serve a master, I did in that moment. I would have kissed his feet, wept for his pleasure, coupled with another pet for his enjoyment, if he took me home and named me his pet. His collar. His tag. A mongrel the honored pet of one of The Guard, owned by one of such unusual coloring...

I'd lied. I hadn't wanted my death. I had wanted *him*. A master or mistress who, when I looked at them, woke my loyalty. Sir Jiat made that part inside me stir, stretch, reach. I didn't want to go back to my cage. I didn't want to wait for death. I wanted to go home with him.

"You may leave, Master Miab." Sir Jiat's voice was a rich, deep purr, rolling through my senses. The moment the door shut, leaving us alone, he crouched in front of me. "You liked looking at me, didn't you, Ewan?"

He'd asked me a question. Did he want me to answer? Was I allowed to speak? I didn't know if he had a cane of his own. I trembled. Should I speak? If I did, should I say yes, I loved looking at him, or should I lie and say no and risk insulting him?

"Speak, Ewan," Sir Jiat said, the words firm but quiet.

"Yes," I rasped out, my throat painfully dry. "You are beautiful. Unusual."

"I am." There was certainty in his voice, and I swore I heard a note of amusement. "Three homes in your life. Did you love your masters?"

Shame bubbled up in me, and I decided not to lie. "Not all of them."

"Good. You're honest. I value honesty. Stand up. I wish to look at you."

I rose at the same time Sir Jiat did, but I kept my eyes averted, my hands loose at my sides. Pets weren't permitted clothing unless snows came, and so I was naked. I could feel his gaze slide over my bare skin, over my arms, legs. He reached out, combed his thick fingers through my matted hair.

"You are filthy." I wanted to protest, to say that as such an old, second-returned pet, I had no right to lovely soaps, clean water, or a comb, but I knew better than to speak. "But, you're strong. Pretty for being such a mutt. You seem well-behaved, but even if you aren't, I believe I could easily train any stubbornness from you. I managed to with my last pet."

I wanted to ask what happened to his previous pet, but I bit my tongue. Sir Jiat circled me, touched my back, my ass, let his claw scrap over the stinging welt Miab had left me with. I whimpered.

"And you're intact. I dislike my males to be anything other than how The Maker intended." Sir Jiat stopped in front of me once more. "Do you wish to come home with me, Ewan?" I trembled, wanting to look up at him again. "Look at me." My eyes snapped up to meet his. "When I ask you a question, you will speak. I want no lies, and I don't like to beat my pets unless my hand is forced. Do not force my hand and you will not be beaten. Now, do you wish to come with me?"

"Yes," I said immediately.

Sir Jiat smiled, and I saw something warm in his eyes then, something that made my gut flutter. "I will fill out the paperwork. You will wait here for my return. I want you to crouch on the balls of your feet, your hands clasped behind your back, your head bowed. Do not move from that position until I come for you."

The position would be painful, would make my legs, back, and shoulders ache, but I'd do it. To go home with him, I'd stand on my damn head. I crouched, grasped my wrist behind my back, and I bowed my head, my stringy brown hair falling into my face. He gave my scalp a little scritch, and then I heard him leave the room. I closed my eyes, forced myself to breathe evenly, and prepared myself for a trial of endurance, as paperwork for a pound adoption could take a whole afternoon to complete.

Sir Jiat took me home. It was a simple as that, it seemed. I'd expected to wait all afternoon as the reams of paperwork were filled out, but Sir Jiat came back for me within the hour. He clipped a leash to my collar and led me out of the pound. The sun was hot, the air thick, and my feet burned as I walked along the white concrete pathway. I was filthy, tired, and shocked I'd been chosen, but as a light breeze blew, carrying with it the distant scent of the sea, I was happy.

Human Rights

He didn't speak to me as he walked from the pound. His carriage was modest, drawn by one small horse, and he tied my leash to one of the posts at the front. He didn't drive his horse hard, but he made me run, the heat of the ground and occasional rock making me wince. I didn't want to let him down or regret choosing me, and so I ran with my head up and my back straight. Not once did he have to yell at me, take the cane to my ass, or slow his carriage. By the time we reached his modest home, I was covered in sweat, my chest heaving as I tried to catch my breath.

Again, he didn't speak. He walked me into the cool shade of his home and handed my leash to a female. She wasn't as finely dressed as Sir Jiat, so I could only assume she was a servant. Her long muzzle and sharp eyes spoke of one of the Jackal breeds, and I thought it strange that one of the Jackals would be employed by one of the Jaguars. The Canines and Felines shared the same world, but they didn't always mix well. It was why, I believed, the political climate was as splintered as it was, for the Felines far outnumbered the Canines, and so the laws benefited the Felines more than the Canines.

I might be nothing more than a pet, but I paid attention. I'd had two Feline masters and one Canine, and the Canines often spoke of their discontent to one another. No one censored themselves around the family pet, after all.

It was then that Sir Jiat turned his full attention to me.

"This is Hosanna. She will be your personal groom. Hosanna has been in my employ for a decade, and she is well-versed in how I expect my pets to behave. If I am not here, her word is law. Do you understand, Ewan?"

The fact that Sir Jiat kept using my name was a marvel. I nodded. "Yes."

"She will take you to the bathing room and properly cleanse you for acceptance in my household. I do not tolerate uncleanliness, and you will be bathed twice a week. Your hair will always be brushed. We will have boots made for you." Sir Jiat looked at Hosanna. "When you're done, bring him into my suite. I will go over the rest of the rules there."

"Yes, Sir," Hosanna said, bowing her head a little. "I will also feed him."

Sir Jiat nodded. "Yes. He is too thin. I doubt that ass at the pound has been properly feeding any of his charges." He seemed to consider me for a moment, and I'd never been more aware of my body and its lack of bulk before. "A filet of chicken, a bowl of those syruped plums Lady Shiall sent over, and three slices of bread from this morning." Sir Jiat turned and started to leave the room, and then he paused and looked over his shoulder with a flick of his tail. "And a glass of milk," he said.

I wanted to drop to my knees again and kiss his sleek, pale feet. It had been several years since I'd had such a lavish meal, and my mouth watered at the mere thought of it. And milk! By the heavens, I'd not had milk in almost a decade. Tears stung my eyes, but I didn't lift my head, didn't speak. After a moment, Sir Jiat left the room, and I was alone with Hosanna. She reached over and lifted my chin until our eyes met.

"Do not avert your eyes in this household. To Sir Jiat, it means shame. Are you ashamed to be his pet?"

"No." I was honored! To be chosen by one of the Elite, to be gifted weekly baths, to be given proper food, it was heavenly. There was nothing here—so far—that brought shame to my heart.

Hosanna grinned, her sharp teeth showing. "Then don't bow your head or avert your eyes unless Sir Jiat commands you to. Come. I have the boiler ready. You are in dire need of a bath. I will tell Werrs to prepare your meal. You can eat while I tend your hair."

By the time I was greedily eating the luscious meal, I was scrubbed clean, my hair and nails trimmed, and my skin oiled to a gleaming bronze. I was proud my bare skin wasn't pasty like many other pets'. I had been kissed by the sun, and Hosanna actually complimented my clear complexion. I even smelled lovely, like oranges and something resinous that made me hum pleasantly whenever I caught wind of myself. As I ate, my belly filling quickly, Hosanna combed my hair, braided it back from my face.

"I've never seen another pet with hair like yours," she said.

I took a deep drink of the cold milk I'd been given. "Like mine?"

"It's thick, but very soft, and from a distance, it looks simply brown. It's not just brown, though. Here in the light, I can see the deep ruddy hue of it. It's quite lovely."

"Thank you," I said, flattered by her compliment.

I finished my meal, feeling bloated and ready for a long nap. When I sat back and sighed, Hosanna chuckled. Her fingers flew through my hair, half of it artfully confined within elaborate braids, the other half left loose. She motioned for me to follow her, and we moved from the bathing room into a richly decorated bedroom. Hosanna told me to kneel on the rug and wait for Sir Jiat's return.

As I sat there, I indulged myself. I looked around.

The colors were deep, dark, masculine. Black, brown, and an emerald green accented the bed, couch, and curtains. I wanted to spread out on the furs covering the bed, curl up and sleep. The food had made me sleepy. But this was my master's room. Pets weren't supposed to be in a master's personal space. At least, none of the masters I'd had before thought a pet's place was beside their master. I was allowed to sleep in the communal rooms or in small houses outside the main house. This was personal. This was *his* room. It smelled of him: his musk and fur.

My knees were aching by the time Sir Jiat entered the room. He sat on the low divan at the foot of the bed, and something glinted in his hand. A collar. It was a beautiful collar, too. Fine tooled leather of a deep green with a shiny silver buckle and leash ring. I licked my lips, and my fingers itched to touch it, to feel the cool leather around my neck. I'd never been gifted with such a fine, unique collar. Mine had always been cheap, itchy, ill-fitting collars my masters had purchased from one of the many shops for pets.

"The tag will be ready to fasten to the ring in a week," Sir Jiat said. "Until then, you will not be allowed out of the house unless you are on a leash and at my heel."

I nodded, unable to take my eyes from the collar. "I understand."

"Good. Come here. Sit on my lap."

He was larger than me, taller and broader, and as I sat upon his lap, I realized how hard and strong his thighs were. He was one of The Guard, and I could see it in every movement, in every muscle. I didn't understand the pull he had on me already. I'd felt it before all the kindnesses, and now that my flesh touched his, I was shocked by the heat that moved through me. I knew the sensation. It was lust. I'd felt it in the past, but I'd never been allowed to sate myself except with my own hand. But to feel lust for one of the masters? It was forbidden. It was grounds to have one's life ended, and after gaining all of this, I didn't want to lose it because my cock was headstrong.

"Head up," Sir Jiat ordered, and my head instantly snapped up, exposing my throat to him. "Do you need a new name, or does Ewan please you?" he asked as he slipped the leather—not too tight, not too loose—around my throat and fastened the buckle.

"The Lady Kica named me Ewan," I said, voice rough.

Sir Jiat chuckled. "I didn't ask who named you. I asked if you liked the name."

I flushed. "No, I don't."

"Do you have a name you like?" Sir Jiat asked, settling the collar, his fingers lingering on my skin. "Did you have a name from the bitch that birthed you?"

I remembered almost nothing about my mother, other than her smell. She'd had an affair with the neighbor's stud. From all accounts, he had held a high pedigree, but she'd been found in the pound. She had been the product of two surrendered pets herself. I was a mutt through and through, but I still remembered her scent. The scent... and the name she called me. I righted my head when Sir Jiat tapped my chin, and I boldly met his beautiful eyes. Still, I hesitated. It was *my* name. I didn't want to give it to him. Not yet.

Sir Jiat smiled, his white, dangerous teeth showing, and he stroked up and down my back. "For now, I think, Ewan will do, won't it?"

S.L. Armstrong

"Yes," I said, arching into his touch. Oh, it felt so good to be touched again! I was clean, fed, and now I was being given such tender attention from my new master. I couldn't help but wonder when the dream would collapse and reality would slap me.

"You will sleep in here, with me, at the foot of my bed," Sir Jiat said, never looking away from my eyes. "I am one of the members of the Human Rights Movement. You will not sleep on the floor. You will not be denied proper food. You will not be denied freedom to move about, to rest, to socialize. You will not be denied clothing in the snows. You are here as my reverent pet, and I will treat you with the utmost respect. Do you understand all that I have said?"

My throat tightened, and my eyes stung as tears gathered. A member of the Human Rights Movement? My new master believed pets to be thinking, feeling creatures worthy of affection and respect? Even the mutts? I swallowed several times, and then bowed my head as I began to weep.

"You do understand," Sir Jiat murmured, cradling me against his body. His large, paw-like hand continued to pet up and down my back, and then his purr burst forth. No master had *ever* purred for me, and I clung to him. It was shameful and disrespectful, but I couldn't help myself. I clung to him and wept as he purred and touched me. "I apologize for my cruelty at the pound, but we act in secret, and men like Miab would never give you over to a master who believed you a thinking, feeling creature. It will not happen again. You begin a new life today, Ewan," he promised me. "A new life."

The first thirty-one years of my life fell away then. I

18

accepted Sir Jiat in that instant, accepted him as my lord and master, my owner, and knew the long years ahead of me would be nothing like the ones that had preceded them. For the first time in my life, I thought myself blessed, and I prayed to whatever might hear me, prayed Sir Jiat would never want to send me back to the pound. I wanted to trust him; I prayed to trust him. As I fell asleep against his shoulder, full and exhausted, I think something must have heard me, because I drifted into dreams with my heart at peace.

Chapter Two

One week later, I stood in the main room, chin lifted, and Sir Jiat fastened my new tag on the ring of my collar. It was official. I was his. No one could deny it now, and I certainly didn't want to. In the course of a week, I'd gained nine pounds, my skin was golden from hours spent in the sun in Sir Jiat's rear yard, and I'd never been as well rested. Nights were spent warm in Sir Jiat's bed. My hair sleek from gentle brushing, my belly full from a day of meals, and my eyelids heavy with exhaustion. Each night, I prayed to know what it was that I'd done to be blessed with such a master.

"I have a surprise for you," Sir Jiat said. I watched him reach for my leash. "There is a meeting of my like-minded associates today. They are bringing their pets with them, and I think it is high time you socialized."

Fear struck me to my core. Socialize? With other pets? I'd never done that before. I was a one-pet home. My previous masters hadn't taken me out. I knew the home, the yard, and the physician's office. The closest I'd come to socialization was peeking through the slats of a fence separating me from another pet or the occasional romp in the pound's lackluster play yard. Socialize? What was expected of me? What was I to do? How was I to ensure I didn't humiliate my master?

Sir Jiat fastened the leash to my collar, and then he brought our eyes together. "I can scent your fear. Do you fear going out? Meeting other owners? Or is it the pets that make you tremble?"

I'd learned, since coming to Sir Jiat's home, that if he asked me questions, he truly wanted my answers. Usually, I didn't hesitate. But I was hesitating, not wanting to ruin his outing. I didn't want to embarrass him, but at the same time, I didn't want to prevent his own ability to socialize with his friends.

"Answer me, Ewan." Sir Jiat's tone was firm, kind, and he gave just the smallest tug on my leash.

"Other than the pound, I've not met other pets. I don't know what it is you will want me to do," I said, heat rising in my cheeks.

Sir Jiat smiled. "I want you to have fun. There is a large yard for you all to run around in, sun yourselves, and Lady Freeya will provide you with delicious things to eat. I want you to have fun."

I tilted my head, unsure. Fun? With other pets?

Shaking his head with a chuckle, Sir Jiat helped me into my sandals. "Fun, Ewan. Where you laugh and talk and play. Nothing more than that. It's casual. There's no need to be nervous, and you won't disappoint me in any way unless you keep yourself apart from everyone. These pets can be your friends, if you let them."

Friends. I knew that word. It was what Kica had called the young women who would visit her home. They'd giggle, talk about some boy or girl in their classes, and eat fattening pastries while grooming their nails. It hadn't seemed like much fun, and when I was allowed to watch, most of what they said to each other seemed disingenuous or cruel. That didn't make me think 'enjoyable' in the slightest. Maybe pets who were friends with one another were different. We didn't have classes or girls and boys to gossip about, though fattening pastries and grooming did sound promising.

"Come now," Sir Jiat said with another tug to my leash. "Let's not keep them waiting too long. You might miss out on some delicious treat or exciting game."

The walk from Sir Jiat's home up into the wealthier homes in the Upper City was pleasant. My feet didn't burn now on the bright pathways, and others didn't pass by and wrinkle their noses. I smelled nice, my body was fuller, and I didn't look like I might be infested with some sort of insect. I held my head up proudly. I couldn't recall the last time I was able to do that. The sense of defeat and resignation I'd felt in my pound cell, waiting for death, had evaporated, and new excitement vibrated through me. I had another forty, perhaps fifty years ahead of me, and if I could stay at Sir Jiat's side—pampered, cared for, and safe—then those years didn't frighten me. What did frighten me was the potential loss of Sir Jiat, Hosanna, and Werrs, of the life I still woke in awe of each morning.

I could hear laughter as we turned down one of the streets, a tall, sand-colored home looming in front of us. It was the largest home I'd ever seen, and the lawn was a bright, fresh green with little yellow flowers speckled through it. It was as welcoming as it was intimidating. I paused at the simple iron gate, swallowing against the fear bubbling in my throat. All my pride faded, replaced with nothing but bitter self-doubt. When my collar bit into my skin as the leash jerked, a soft whine filled my throat. I no longer felt safe and warm and content. I was cold. My skin prickled as each hair stood on end, and my gut roiled anxiously. I didn't want to go in there. I didn't want to be petted by other masters, and I didn't want to play with other pets. I wanted to go *home*.

Home. How odd Sir Jiat's residence already was home to me. I'd never been so settled so quickly before. The cool shade and dark, rich colors of Sir Jiat's room called to me. I wanted to run back home and hide from this, but Sir Jiat gave another, more impatient, tug to my leash, and the whine was finally given voice. I stared with wide eyes at the impressive home, and my feet simply wouldn't budge. I was frozen, much to my master's dismay.

"Ewan." Sir Jiat forced our eyes to meet. "We are expected, and it's rude to keep my friends waiting. Come inside. There is nothing to fear."

I swallowed thickly. "I'm afraid."

Sir Jiat reached out and scratched me sweetly behind my ear. "I know, but if you take the steps necessary, you will find there is nothing to be frightened of. You are not the eldest pet, and you are not the only mutt." His muzzle split in an amused smile. "Though, I must say, I think you the most beautiful."

The compliment brought a blush to my cheeks. Sir Jiat had not called me beautiful yet, and I certainly had never expected him to. I ducked my head and stepped forward, now more willing to follow him into the house. If he thought me the most beautiful, then I would make him proud of my beauty, allow him to showcase it without complaint. Sir Jiat knocked, and he was almost immediately let inside. While I was allowed to lift my head in Sir Jiat's home, I was ushered into a nobleman's home, and I didn't know if I was permitted to look around. My fear rose hot and sharp in me, my gut roiling from nerves. What I supposed to do? Where was I supposed to look? By the stars, I was going to be sick!

"Ewan."

My master's voice made it through the haze of panic, and I righted my head without a thought. His honey-orange eyes filled my vision, and I calmed almost instantly. Sir Jiat motioned to the other figure in the entryway.

"Hyra, this is Ewan."

The female was from the Lynx breed, and she was sleek and lovely, her eyes bright. She smiled, her whiskers twitching as she scented the air around us. "There's nothing to be afraid of," she said, holding out her hand. Sir Jiat unclipped my leash, and I took her hand. "The other pets are in the yard. I'm certain they'd love to meet you."

I followed her, my heart pounding, and I glanced over my shoulder to make sure Sir Jiat was following us. Even with him, my fear didn't fully ease. How many of these pets waited? Was I to speak to them? Sir Jiat had said I could eat and play, but what did pets play? At the pound, we merely chased one another trying to stretch our muscles after a week confined to our cages. Games weren't for the castoffs, and I didn't know if these pets would be willing to teach me. I might not be the oldest, but I was older, and what group of playful pets would want to teach a four-home mongrel their games?

Hyra opened a pair of doors that led out into a very green yard. It was an intense contrast to all the pale homes around it. I blinked a few times, and then the seven pets came into my line of sight. They were chasing balls and laughing, kicking the balls back and forth, and they looked so happy. Fit. Their skin golden and their hair well-groomed. I looked up at Sir Jiat, unsure, but I was less afraid now. I wanted to rush out, learn their games with the balls, and roll about in the grass that looked thick and soft.

"Go on," Sir Jiat said. "I will call you when it's time to go home."

I bit my lip, hesitating, but Sir Jiat gave me a pat on my ass, and I rushed out into the yard, the sun warm on my skin. The other pets stopped, their eyes on me, looking me up and down. I stopped about a dozen steps from them, and I looked over my shoulder, but the door to the house was shut and my master was gone. The fear gnawed at me again. My eyes met one of the female's—she had lovely green eyes that the grass complemented perfectly—and she grinned at me.

"My name's Victoria," the green-eyed female said, all but hopping over to me in her excitement. "Are you Sir Jiat's new pet?"

I nodded. "My name's Ewan."

One of the males, who looked no more than sixteen, rushed over. "Ewan? What a fun name! I'm Marc."

"Marc and Victoria," I said, trying to cement their names in my mind.

One by one, I was introduced to the other five: David, Jill, Shale, Nadia, and Cal. Cal was the oldest of us, having just turned fifty, and Marc the youngest at seventeen. I smiled as they clamored to tell me all about their lives, how each of them had been saved from the pound by their masters. Their stories were so much like mine, except for Jill. She was a purebreed, and she didn't want to talk much about how her mistress, the Lady Hyra I'd met when I'd come into the house, had come to own her.

I didn't care. I wanted to know all about those bright balls and the game they'd been playing.

"Football," Cal said. "We use five balls and kick them back and forth. You never know who's going to have the ball or who will kick it your way. If you miss a kick, you have to do six somersaults before joining in again."

A new flush made its way to my cheeks. "I don't know what a somersault is."

Jill gasped. "You don't?"

I shook my head. "My previous masters didn't play with me. Not... not like this," I said, gesturing to the yard with its balls, metal climbing jungle, and small pond. It was heavenly, and I almost envied Jill her luck, but I wouldn't give Sir Jiat up for the most exciting yard in all the world.

"We'll show you," Shale said, his body the most muscled out of everyone else's. "You crouch down like this," he said, showing me how to crouch. I followed his example. "Hold your hands up by your head, tuck your head over, and then push."

I watched Shale roll feet over head, and then pop back up with a grin. Oh! That looked like such fun. It took me four false starts—and a lot of cheering from the pets—before I managed my first somersault. It was as fun as it looked, and I thought, even if I missed a kick or six, I wouldn't mind if I could do that again.

Outside in the sunshine, food and water freely available, I played for the first time in my life. I chased Cal and Jill through the yard. Shale showed me how to climb the metal jungle. I kicked the balls around with everyone else, missing so many times, I was laughing and dizzy by the time I collapsed in a heap with Jill, Marc, and Victoria. The laughter was wonderful, and the comfort I felt as Victoria combed her fingers through my hair was unimaginable. Never had I dared to wish for this, wish for joy and sides aching from expressing my pleasure.

The sun was high and hot, and after all the activity, I was sleepy. I thought Jill might go for her mistress, who could then call for Sir Jiat to take me home, but no one got up. We slaked our thirst with the pitchers of cool water, and then curled up in a great naked, sweaty pile under a large oak tree. The shade was just cool enough to be comfortable, and Jill laid in front of me while Marc took up a position behind. His body was pleasantly broad against my back, and Jill was soft in my arms. It was heavenly, and I fell asleep within moments.

A chilled breeze woke me. I blinked several times, cozy amid the warm, naked bodies around me, and another breeze—cool and damp—kissed my flesh. The sun had disappeared behind gray clouds, and the could smell the oncoming storm. Jill shifted in my arms, her body moving against mine, and to my shame, my sex hardened. I couldn't help the whimper in my throat, and it woke Jill. Her bright eyes, blue and clear, met mine, and a flush crept over her cheeks. I couldn't hide. I couldn't move. She was in front of me, and Marc was still plastered to my back. I didn't know what I was supposed to do, and then lightning split the sky, followed by a loud, dangerous rumble of thunder.

The group roused themselves, and Jill eased her body from mine, but it only bared my shame to everyone. I drew in on myself, wishing away the hardness between my thighs. It was wrong, so wrong, and before I knew it, I was weeping. Sir Jiat would surely punish me now. I'd embarrassed him. As soon as Jill told her mistress, I would be beaten, sent back to the pound, a disappointment, and I would lose all I'd only just begun to taste. I couldn't help my tears, and remained out in the grass beneath the oak tree even as the rains began to fall.

All the bright laughter and easy warmth from earlier in the afternoon washed away under the cool summer rain. I would have willingly stayed out there, my pulse pounding in my groin, but just as thunder rolled through the sky again, a hand threaded through my hair. That hand was insistent, turning my wet face up, and Sir Jiat's worried expression filled my vision. Behind him was the Lady Hyra, holding a large umbrella over us all. As soon as I saw him, a master already beloved to me, I wept anew, the sobs deep and contrite. He gathered me into his arms, and I saw his eyes dart to my groin, and I wanted to push him away, continue to hide my shame, but he hefted me up and, with Lady Hyra leading the way, took me into the dry warmth of Lady Hyra's home.

I buried my face against Sir Jiat's shoulder. He was soaking wet because of me. I began to shiver in his arms, and I expected to be tossed to the floor, flogged for ruining everything. Instead, I heard a door shut, and the sound of running water overtook the soft patter of rain. I dared to lift my head, and I saw a tub of steaming water. Looking around, I saw no one in the bathing room but us, and I blinked several times, confused. Sir Jiat set me into the hot water, and I hissed as it engulfed my sex, which was finally beginning to soften. After a moment, Sir Jiat lifted my head and washed my face with a warm, soft washcloth.

"Would you like to tell me what is the matter?" Sir Jiat asked, his voice so gentle as to bring new tears to my eyes.

"F-Forgive me," I all but sobbed.

S.L. Armstrong

Sir Jiat smiled. "Forgive you? What for?"

"I shamed myself with the other pets!" I couldn't lie to him. I wouldn't. If there was to be a punishment, I would meet it with the truth on my lips.

"Shamed yourself? How, Ewan? It looked to me as if you enjoyed an active afternoon and a long nap." Sir Jiat began to wash me himself. It was such an honor, and I could barely enjoy it.

I looked down into the soapy water. "My cock," I whispered. "It grew hard." I knew from experience that such a thing happening when I wasn't alone was a terrible sin. All my previous masters would beat me for the offense.

"That happens." Sir Jiat forced our eyes to meet. "It is the natural order of things. You were just waking, you had a beautiful female before you, a lovely male behind. They were not offended. I am not offended. Marc and Shale were just as erect as you. Why would you think it shameful?"

I shifted in the water. "My previous masters would beat me if I hardened where any could see."

"Well, that is their sin, not yours." Sir Jiat began washing my hair, and the chill of the rain and my fear began to fade. "I will never beat you for your body doing as nature intended it to. Have you ever fucked a female?" My eyes, large and shocked, must have been answer enough for him because Sir Jiat laughed. "I see. No, you haven't. I will find a suitable female for you to spend yourself with. No intact male pet should go his life without proper, frequent relief."

Sir Jiat washed me, warmed me, soothed me. There was no beating, no harsh words. It was as confusing to me as anything in my life now. Since Sir Jiat had chosen me, nothing had been as I'd expected, and I didn't quite know what to do with it. As he dried me off, humming softly, I relaxed, trusted him, and by the time he led me out of the bathroom and into the playroom where the other pets were enjoying hot soup, I'd calmed completely. I was welcomed back among the pets, offered a bowl of the thick soup, and then left by my master to socialize with my new friends.

It was yet another of the best days of my life, and I would forever remember it. My first real day in the world, with others like myself and a master who promised me no beatings for simply being a male with his genitals completely whole still. I grinned as I dug into the soup, listening to David talk about how excited he was that the next play day would be at his master's home.

To my surprise, Sir Jiat smiled at me from the doorway. The look in his beautiful eyes, the split of his muzzle, made my heart jump in my chest. That smile told me I would be going to that play day, too, and I found myself smiling back at him until he pushed off from the doorway and disappeared down the hall. David nudged me, and I laughed and pounced on him, wrestling with him across the floor as the others cheered us on.

It was the best day in my life, and the memory of Sir Jiat's smile promised me many more.

S.L. Armstrong

Chapter Three

I had been promised an opportunity to rut, but I hadn't thought beyond the initial offer. My focus was on each day, pleasing Sir Jiat and being as good a pet as I could be. I didn't want to be sent back to the pound, and the longer I remained with Sir Jiat, the less likely that seemed. Still, it was a thought that would wake me in a cold sweat in the depths of the night. I would jerk awake at the foot of Sir Jiat's bed, chilled by the memories of being nothing more than meat ready for the slaughter. My throat would be so dry, I would swear I wouldn't be able to swallow at all, but I was afraid to leave the bed. I shouldered my discomfort, shifted at my master's feet, and would chase sleep until the sun kissed the sky.

This morning, Sir Jiat had left me lazing in bed. I had protested as best I could without being insolent, but he would hear none of it.

"You look tired," Sir Jiat said. "You need your rest."

I sat up, my joints aching from exhaustion. "I can rest in the afternoon when you make your rounds at the Guardhouse."

Sir Jiat shook his head, using a brush to fluff up the fur of his tail. His ears were slightly back, and I knew that meant he was unhappy. I didn't want him unhappy, and so I slid from the bed and crawled to him. My knees screamed at me, but I remained elegant, gliding on my hands and knees. I took the brush from him and set to grooming his beautiful, white fur.

"I have begged off my turn today at the Guardhouse." Sir Jiat watched me in the mirror. "I arranged for a friend of mine to bring her pet. Syra is a lovely woman, older and sterile, but I think she will be an ideal match for your first."

My hands stopped moving mid-brushing, and fear coiled around my heart. My master had found a female for me, and I didn't know what I was supposed to do with her. I knew the basic idea. Cock into slit. Beyond that, though, I was lost. I shifted on my knees, trying to finish grooming Sir Jiat before he received company, but I was distracted. Adrift. Today, I would rut with a woman, and I was scared. He must have smelled the fear because he knelt in front of me, cupping my cheek with his large, paw-like hand.

"Do you not want Syra?" he asked.

I gripped the brush so hard, I felt the sharp bristles break the skin of my palm. Gasping, I dropped the brush, and then I immediately dove after it, ashamed for letting it fall. "Forgive me!"

Sir Jiat gripped my shoulders and forced me to meet his amber eyes. "Ewan, you've hurt yourself." He opened my palm, smeared with red and dozens of little pinpricks. It stung like fire. "You must take care." Sir Jiat then did something I had never, in my wildest dreams, expected: he bent his head and drew his rough, hot tongue over my broken flesh. Each swipe cleaned a little more blood from my palm. I couldn't help but whimper. "Why are you afraid?" he asked, his ears twitching on the top of his head, attentive.

It took me a few moments to force my throat to work, my tongue to form words. "I don't know what I should do," I admitted.

A smile graced Sir Jiat's face, sharp teeth showing as his whiskers twitched. "I see. It isn't difficult. You will grow erect, she will lay back, and you will slide into her body."

"And then?" I looked up, flushed with embarrassment. It was personal, intimate, but I had no secrets from my master.

"You thrust in and out until you come." Sir Jiat rose from the cushioned seat in front of the vanity. "Come with me. I will bathe you myself before Syra arrives. She is experienced. Put your trust in her to guide you through this. There is no need for shame."

I followed Sir Jiat obediently, watching his white tail twitch as he walked. Even if there was no need for shame, I felt it. I was a mutt. No one bred mutts, and if we had needs, they were trivial. To be given an opportunity to know such pleasures even once was something I'd never dared to hope for. But, Sir Jiat said it would become a weekly arrangement. Not always Syra, but someone. I would never be forced to go without so long as I was obedient, and as Sir Jiat rinsed my hair of soap, I swore to never disobey him. I didn't *want* to disobey him. So long as I obeyed, I would be kept, and maybe the nightmares would lessen.

In the warmth of the morning, with Sir Jiat's hands moving slickly over my body, those night frights seemed distant. The heat of the bath eased my sore joints, and Sir Jiat's gentle touch stirred my body and heart. As I grew hard in the bath, Sir Jiat chuckled and called me eager. He promised Syra would arrive soon. I smiled bashfully, unwilling to correct him. It wasn't Syra's hands on my body now. It wasn't Syra's kindness that kept my belly full, my body clean, and my mind challenged. It wasn't Syra's amber eyes I wanted to gaze up into and see bright with pleasure. I wondered if Sir Jiat would purr if touched just right, what his fur would feel like under a lustful touch.

But those desires were forbidden. To want and lay with one's master only led to the pound and that back room where the guilty found their end. We ignored my erection as Sir Jiat honored me by drying my body, and then he brushed my hair. If I could have purred, I would have. Pampered and adored, my heart slowed, my fears eased. It took all I had not to reach out for Sir Jiat, to touch him freely. I was well-trained, and I resisted. I merely stood in the bathing room, clean and groomed, all but preening under Sir Jiat's attention.

"Beautiful." Sir Jiat slid his hand from my neck down to my hip. "I wish I could have found you years ago before your previous masters had chipped away at you."

I tilted my head. "Chipped away at me? I don't understand."

Sir Jiat smiled as the door chimes sounded. "Don't worry about it. Come with me. We will greet Cana and her pet."

Cana, it turned out, wasn't a noble. She also wasn't one of the Felines. She was one of the Wolves. Syra, her pet, was older than me, but she was pretty with long, golden hair and pert breasts. I wasn't sure if I was supposed to bow at Cana, touch Syra, or wait for Sir Jiat to order me to fuck her. The calm I'd managed to gain in the bathing room was lost the moment we stepped into the foyer and faced Cana and Syra. I bowed my head to hide my flush, and I shifted from one foot to the other.

"Sir Jiat." Cana leaned forward and brushed her cheek against Sir Jiat's. "I'm honored you have invited us into your home."

"The honor is all mine, Cana." Sir Jiat ushered us out of the foyer and into the main living space. A cool breeze blew through the room from the open windows as Sir Jiat and Cana sat on the long sofa while Syra and I sat on the floor at our masters' feet. "Syra is agreeable?"

Cana reached out and stroked her fingers through Syra's hair. Syra closed her eyes and made a happy sound in the back of her throat. That was the sound Sir Jiat made me want to make! "She is. She's excited. Being older, not many masters or mistresses seek us out as an intimate companion possibility, even for one night."

Sir Jiat shift, bringing Syra's attention to him. "You understand that Ewan is new to this? That his previous masters were uncaring of such needs?"

Syra nodded. "Yes, Sir Jiat. I understand."

"And you will be careful with him?"

Now Syra smiled, a blush stealing over her golden cheeks. "Yes, Sir Jiat."

Sir Jiat pressed a kiss to my brow, and then called for Hosanna. "Please take them into the third bedroom, and then bring refreshments for Cana and me." He smiled at Cana. "We have a lot of catching up to do."

Cana laughed softly. "Yes, we do."

An odd feeling of jealousy moved through me as I saw them share an intimate look. I didn't understand it, and I had little time to think about it as Hosanna motioned for Syra and me to follow her. I was frowning when I stepped into the bedroom. It was a simple guest room decorated in white and seafoam, comfortable and bright. Hosanna closed the door. Suddenly, I was alone with Syra, a woman I had met but a handful of minutes ago. She tucked a lock of hair behind her ear, hugged herself, and then smiled at me.

"You're nervous."

I couldn't help but smile in return. "Very."

"You don't need to be. I understand. Cana was the first master to allow me freedom with my body. She found me my first male to lay with, much like Sir Jiat found me for you." Syra stepped forward, drew her fingers across my shoulder and down my arm. "Am I pleasing to look at?"

I looked her up and down, from the swell of her breasts to the curve of her hips. She was lovely. Healthy. She wasn't too large or too thin. Her hair was beautiful, and I ran my fingers through the thick curtain of it. Like silk. I closed what space remained between us. "You are very pleasing," I murmured. "I just don't know what to do. Not really."

Syra's smile became something seductive, alluring, and she slipped her hand into mine. A moment's pause, and then she led me to the bed. She climbed atop the fine fabrics draping the soft mattress and tugged my hand. I joined her, kneeling in the center of the bed as her hands moved over my chest, down my stomach. I groaned. That touch was unlike any handling I'd had before, soft and tempting, setting my body on fire in its wake. I grew stiff between my legs, and when she bent to press her lips to the head of me, I thought I'd die from the pleasure of it.

She straightened, cupped my face, and brought our lips together. First, it was merely our lips against each other, and then her tongue touched my lips. I gasped, and her tongue went from touching my lips to tasting my mouth. It was wicked, wet and slick, and I hesitated only a moment before my hands stroked down her back, cupped her ass, and pulled her against me. Instinct woke in me, and as we kissed, I pressed her to the bed. Need burned in me, hot and heavy and overwhelming, as she parted her thighs and I rested against her.

Syra's hands grabbed my ass, pulled me closer, and my cock rubbed against the wet slit of her. The need compounded within me. I tried thrusting forward, but I wasn't lined up right. I tried a second time, a growl fed into our kiss. Still, I couldn't push inside! Syra broke the kiss, panting, and reached down between us. There was no annoyance in her eyes, no cruelty, only the same burning desire that raged inside me. She took me in hand and pressed the head of my cock to her opening, and the moment I felt that slight give, I surged forward. My shout of triumph was joined by her cry of pleasure, and the slick heat around my shaft almost drove me mad.

I didn't know anything more than what Sir Jiat had told me: thrust until the pleasure was too much, and then spend myself within Syra. The thought of Sir Jiat, of his beautiful eyes and soft, white fur made my heart race with those forbidden thoughts once again. It wasn't fair to Syra, either. I should be thinking of her as I rocked in and out, but the more I tried to focus on the grip of her hands, the clinging wetness around my cock, and the teeth at my throat, the more my thoughts turned to Sir Jiat. How did males fuck? How would it feel to thrust into him... or him into me? Would his teeth be as sharp as they looked, or would he be gentle with me? Would his tail thump against the bed or wrap around my body?

S.L. Armstrong

"Ewan!" Syra gasped against my ear, the quick, moist sound of our bodies rushing back to me. "So thick... by the gods, yes, like that!"

At least I was doing well. I was doing it right. There was no mistake; it felt good, but it wasn't all I'd thought it would be. I thrust hard, fast, urged by Syra's hands and her cries. The pleasure built to a fevered pitch, and then my body jerked, trembled as a choked cry fell from my lips. It was all the wonderful things in my life: the heat of the sun, the warmth of grass, the sweet tang of a summer berry. I would never forget that feeling, the rush it brought as my balls emptied their seed into Syra's quivering body. Her nails raked down my back, and I hissed as I rode out her bucking and squirming.

We panted, glued together in those moments by musk and fluids and sweat. Syra wore a dazed, pleased expression, and as my cock ceased its spasms, a heaviness fell upon me. I wanted to roll over and sleep the afternoon away, and since Sir Jiat hadn't told me I couldn't, I did just that. I withdrew myself and flopped beside her on the soft bed, and her arms embraced me as she curled against my body. It was pleasant enough, enjoyable. Still, as my heart slowly calmed in my chest, it felt off. Something was missing. Something hadn't been quite right. I knew what it was as I nuzzled Syra's head. Syra wasn't Sir Jiat. Sir Jiat was the one my thoughts turned to in that moment of pleasure, but that desire was forbidden. I would never know how Sir Jiat's tongue would feel against my skin, or if Sir Jiat purred in the aftermath of release.

It was with Sir Jiat's eyes in my mind that I fell into dreams. Dreams littered with white fur, a soft, wet nose, and a rumbling purr that put my fears to rest. When I woke, I was alone in the bed, my body aching with need once more. I remained there until the worst of the hardness abated, and then I rose from the bed and padded out into the hallway. The shadows were long, the house quiet. My feet carried me silently from the guest bedroom to the master bedroom, and I paused outside the half-closed door. Was I supposed to come looking for Sir Jiat? Or was I to remain in the other bedroom? I shifted from foot to foot, uncertain.

"Come in, Ewan."

Sir Jiat's voice, that deep almost-growl, wrapped around me, and I pushed into the room. He was alone on his bed, tail curled around him as he paged through a book. I couldn't read, but some nights, Sir Jiat read to me. I paused at the foot of his bed. "I didn't know if I should stay in the other bedroom, Master."

His muzzle cracked into a smile. "Only if you don't want to sleep with me after your first tumble."

I shook my head. "No. I don't want to sleep alone." I climbed onto the bed, settled under the blankets at the footboard. "If I may ask, where is Syra?"

The fluffy white tip of Sir Jiat's tail twitched against the counterpane. "You were sleeping soundly, and Cana had to return home to her husband. You will see Syra again. Cana will bring her back in six days."

Another afternoon with Syra. I shifted on the bed, fidgeting with a loose thread on the counterpane. As much as I appreciated Sir Jiat's offer, I didn't want another afternoon with a female I didn't know. I wanted *him*. I looked up at Sir Jiat. "I... forgive me, and I don't mean offense, but..."

Sir Jiat reached out and let his hand run down my back. "Tell me, Ewan. No need to fear."

"I don't want to fuck Syra again." A flush moved warmly over my face. "I mean no disrespect—"

"Did you not like her?"

I looked up at my master, confused. "It was... pleasurable. Enjoyable. But... it wasn't..." How did I explain that it wasn't soft, smooth skin and gentle curves that now haunted my mind? The heat and need I'd felt was similar to the heat and need I'd felt in the bath before Syra's arrival. That heat had been wonderful, intoxicating with Sir Jiat, but with Syra, it hadn't been *right*. "It wasn't what I'd thought it would be. I would rather not do it again and disappoint Syra."

Sir Jiat stroked down my back again, tender and sweet. The touch thrilled me. "All right." He smiled at me. "Should you find yourself in need, tell me, understood?"

I curled up at his feet, and he continued to pet me. "I understand."

"Would you like me to read to you?"

Warmth filled me. "Yes, please, Master." I closed my eyes, and his voice rumbled around me, deep and true. As I drifted in and out, barely hearing the story he read to me, I knew I was truly safe. My desire was mine, kept buried inside me, my own special love for my master, and I was content with that. That night, my dreams were quiet, still, and I slept as I hadn't in a long, long time.

Chapter Four

By the time fall had come to the city, I'd settled into a routine in which I thrived. Once a week, Sir Jiat took me to a different home where he would meet with other Felines and Canines while I played in the dying heat of summer. I always spent time with the same pets: Victoria, Mar, David, Jill, Shale, Nadia, and Cal. Today, though, we didn't go out. Hosanna busied herself around Sir Jiat's home, cleaning every surface until it sparkled, and then cooked up a banquet of delicious smelling foods. Sir Jiat saw to me himself. That happened more and more. My weekly baths had once been handled by Hosanna, but now Sir Jiat bathed me.

"Are we not going to Lady Hyra's home?" I asked as he rinsed my hair. The questions came easier with each passing day, and I reveled in the freedom.

Sir Jiat shook his head. "No. We will go to Lady Hyra's home in two weeks' time. Today, everyone is coming here. It's why Hosanna has been so busy with preparations."

Excitement bubbled in me. We were going to have guests! A handful of months ago, that would have terrified me, but now I was all but bouncing in the bath. "Where will all the pets go?"

"It's much too cold for you all to play outside, and I

know my courtyard is not nearly as nice as those who have more gold than I, so everyone will remain inside. Hosanna has cleaned out that third bedroom, leaving it clear for you all to play with the toys in there." Sir Jiat drained the tub and reached for a towel. "Come now." He smiled at me, his amber eyes glittering pleasantly. "Time for grooming."

Grooming was my favorite activity with Sir Jiat. Well, aside for the nights when he'd let me lay my head in his lap so he could pet me as he read aloud. Those were the best times. The grooming was a close second. I stood on a mat that absorbed all the extra water that dripped from me as Sir Jiat's hands moved over me with the towel. From head to toe, he dried me with gentle touches, and I lamented yet again that I couldn't purr like the Felines. Still, I smiled, remaining still for him. When every drop of water had been soaked up, Sir Jiat picked up the jar of sweet smelling oils I loved so much. The scent of olive and orange, bright and sharp, filled the steamy air as he began to rub it into my skin. Feet to ankles. Ankle to calves. Calves to knees and thighs. This was the hardest part for me. His large hands, the pads of his fingers and palms so soft, moving over my oil-slicked skin was so erotic that it took all I had to keep from growing hard.

I used to think that once he passed my balls, cock, and ass that the arousal would die. That it would be easier. But even his hands on my back or stomach would make lust rise up inside me, twist my insides up. Sir Jiat had to know. There was no way that my scent remained the same, that he didn't feel the tension singing in my muscles under his hands. Still, he never brought attention to my struggles, never made me flush with shame by pointing out my weakness.

Human Rights

Sir Jiat spread some of the oil into my hair, and then dragged a comb through it. Oh, if only I could purr, but instead, I moaned. It was as close to purring as I could manage, and the comb pulling gently through my oiled hair was just heavenly. All I wanted to do by the time Sir Jiat set the comb aside was collapse in a puddle of wobbly pleasure. Sir Jiat wiped his hands, chuckling as he watched me sway on my feet. I felt my cheeks heat lightly. "It's pleasant," I said, grinning as I defended myself.

"Yes, it is. You look ready for a nap, not an afternoon of play." Sir Jiat shook his head, smiling as he padded out of the bathroom. "Come along, Ewan. Our guests will arrive, and it is up to you to take the pets back to the room where you can all play. Remember to keep your voices down as we are indoors."

I chased after my master, the heaviness leaving my limbs as responsibility was foisted upon them. "I promise to keep everyone quiet."

"Not quiet, just no screaming or loud bursts of laughter. I'd rather we not draw attention to us."

Before I could hold my tongue, I blurted out, "Because you are all part of the Human Rights Movement."

Sir Jiat stopped in his tracks and turned to face me. His face was so fierce, I found myself cowering. "Do not speak so easily those words in this city," he warned. "There are eyes and ears everywhere, my sweet Ewan, and they would have your life and my hide should they know a Guard supports the Movement."

"Yes, Master," I whispered, tears stinging my eyes. I was so stupid, taking liberties I shouldn't. It was so easy to venture down that path, though. First the ability to give truthful answers, and then the right to ask questions. But I had never been given the privilege of speaking out of turn. "I'm sorry."

"Ewan." Sir Jiat sighed, his tailing twitching in a way that spoke of his uncertainty. "I just want you to be aware of the consequences. Within these walls, some questions can be asked without fear, but others... even those must be carefully worded."

I looked up at him. "I don't understand." That was a common state for me, quite honestly. I might pay attention to my surroundings, catch on to what those around me were talking about, but the ramifications... those were beyond me most times. "Why can't we talk about it freely?"

"Because speech comes at a price." Sir Jiat cupped my cheek. "I don't want you to become a casualty to my crusade."

That didn't help me understand, but it did make heat move through me. I was important to him. I wasn't *just* a pet. I meant enough for him to want nothing bad to happen to me because of his own actions. A smile curved my lips. "I trust you."

Sir Jiat's ears twitched, his tail stilling. "I hope I don't make you regret trusting me," he murmured, and I was about to ask how he could possibly make me regret that when the door chime rang. "Our friends arrive. Let us greet them, Ewan."

"Yes, Master." I followed closely, the earlier excitement returning as the door opened to reveal Lord Shal and Marc. While Sir Jiat and Lord Shal greeted each other, spoke in soft voices, I took Marc by the hand and led him deeper into the house, toward the cleared room. "Welcome to Sir Jiat's home," I said, grinning from ear to ear.

Marc looked around the large, mostly empty room.

"Very nice. Shal's home is in the wealthy district, but it's small."

I flushed brightly. "You use your master's name so casually."

"He told me to." Marc laughed, flopping back onto the soft rug in the center of the room. "Hasn't Sir Jiat given you the same permission?"

"No." I sat down on the floor, legs folded under me. "But he allows me freedom to speak, to ask questions."

Marc smiled at me. "And how many questions have you asked?"

I stared at my feet. "Not many. I still don't feel it's my place to question my master."

"If he told you it was all right, you should take him at his word." Marc nudged me with a toe. "Don't you trust your master?"

"I do—" The door chime rang again. "Oh! I'll be right back. Sir Jiat said I was to greet all the pets." I stood and rushed from the room. Back and forth I went as the room slowly filled with the other pets. There were more than any time before. Usually, there were only ever eight or nine of us, but soon, there were eighteen pets packed into the room. I didn't know half of the pets, and I fidgeted a lot, keeping close to Marc and Nadia.

Nadia nuzzled my shoulder. "It's all right," she whispered. "We're all here because our masters see us as more than pets."

"I don't understand," I whispered back. "Why all these meetings?"

"It's so we all grow to know one another, trust each other," Marc said. "When the meeting is over, and we've all gone home, ask Sir Jiat to explain. He may just be waiting for you to ask the questions. For now..." He ran over to a rack of brightly colored balls. "Let's play Colors!"

A cry of excitement rose in the room, and though I tried to quiet them, it was useless. After a few moments, I didn't care. I was laughing with the rest of them as we played with the balls, an intricate game involving colors, goals, and tagging. The room was just large enough for us all to enjoy the game, then a meal, and then a nap. The nap was the best, all of us laying about, cuddled close, and as I drifted off, I was so happy, I didn't want the day to end.

But it did end. After the nap, we had one more game of Colors before the masters and mistresses collected their pets. One by one, I watched my friends—because they were my friends now. I had friends!—wave and leave. Another week until I would see them all again, and it seemed like such a long time away. Still, I was all smiles when Sir Jiat came for me, the house silent as Hosanna began the long process of cleaning up after pets and masters alike. Sir Jiat led me into his room, and he began to undress, tossing the used clothing into a basket.

Sir Jiat was unusually quiet, his ears back and tail still. He was unhappy. All I had to do was see his limp tail to know he was very unhappy. Why would he be unhappy? And then my heart dropped. We hadn't been quiet. Oh, no, I hadn't kept everyone quiet, and I was surely in trouble now. I swallowed against the lump in my throat. "I'm sorry," I rasped out.

"Sorry?" Sir Jiat lifted his head, those eyes sharp on me. "What are you sorry for?"

A blush rushed across my cheeks, down my throat. "I—I didn't keep... keep everyone quiet. We were too loud. I'm sorry I failed. It was a simple task, and I failed." I looked away, hoping he wouldn't see the tears in my eyes. "Will you beat me now?"

Sir Jiat growled low in his throat. "Beat you?"

"I... didn't obey."

"Beat you? Because you and your friends were enjoying yourselves?"

I looked up slowly, so confused. "But I disobeyed."

He sighed and walked into the bathing room, opening the taps to fill the tub with hot water. I followed, unsure. "I'm not going to beat you, Ewan, now or ever," Sir Jiat said, standing and facing me. "That isn't what this is about."

"You're unhappy." I shifted on my feet. "Why are you unhappy?" I asked. It was a small question, a simple question, and I dipped my toes into those waters, hoping not to drown.

"We lost a member of our organization this past week." He shut off the taps and stepped into the steaming bath. "Magistrate Chiaran, someone who was instrumental in our attempts to legislate human rights, fell from his roof two days ago. We lose so much ground with his death."

I had met Magistrate Chiaran once, several weeks ago, when he'd come to visit Sir Jiat. It saddened me that the jovial, tall Lion would never again laugh in my presence. I crossed the room to kneel beside Sir Jiat's tub. "I'm sorry he's gone," I murmured. "I liked his laugh."

Sir Jiat's hand reached out and cupped my face, a sad smile on his. "He had a good laugh and a good heart. I am certain there is another Magistrate that will help our cause, but I will miss Chiaran."

I turned my face into his touch, kissed his palm reverently. My master's heart hurt, and I wished I could heal it just a little. I had so many questions, and I hadn't been reprimanded for my first one, so I chose another. "I don't understand the full purpose of the Human Rights Movement. Victoria once told me that it was a movement of Felines and Canines that..." I blushed, not wanting to compliment my own species so brazenly, even if they had been Victoria's words.

"Tell me what Victoria said," Sir Jiat urged. "I know there is a question brewing in you, so out with it all, my sweet Ewan."

The way he said my name, calling me his, calling me sweet, made the blush all the deeper. "She told me that those who were a part of the Movement thought we shouldn't be bred and kept as pets. That... those of the Movement thought us intelligent, thought we should be equals." I tilted my head a little. "Is that what it is? Is that... how you see me?"

Sir Jiat leaned back against the rest of the tub. "Yes, in the simplest terms. Humans are enslaved. Beaten. Treated as nothing but prizes for our kind to own. It may have always been so, but just because it's always been doesn't mean it must always be." He cupped the water, let it slip through his fingers. "The Movement seeks to legislate equality. Free those who wish to be free, protect those who wish to remain owned. We want to see choice given to all Humans." His slitted eyes turned to me, and my heart began to pound. "We want to be able to love Humans as we love each other."

I shook my head, breathing quickly. "That is a crime. That will bring about any pet's death!"

Something shifted in Sir Jiat's gaze, but I didn't understand what I was looking at. "Sometimes, death must be risked to achieve progress. Outside this city, there is a colony, Ewan. It has Felines and Canines making lives side by side with Humans. No one is owned. There are no pets, no collars, nothing but love and determination to make a better world for ourselves and our children. The law in this city does not reach the colony, and while lawmakers here wish to keep silent the existence of the colony, many of us know of it. Many of us want to live there ourselves, but some must remain here to help change the laws."

"But, *how*?" My brow furrowed. How could a whole colony exist and no pet know of it? "How can such a place be?"

Sir Jiat smiled at me, an indulgent, soft smile. "Where there is a will, sweet Ewan, there is a way. As needed, we leave this city and never come back. But until circumstances dictate, we remain here, making changes where we can."

"And the meetings?"

"It is one small part of the whole. Such meetings happen all over the city, and word travels between each group. Ewan, it's about *change*. It has to start somewhere, and we've chosen to start that change with all of us." Sir Jiat sat up in the water so he could face me. "None of us force our pets to *be* pets. You are all loved, cared for, treated as much of an equal as we can without drawing eyes our way."

What he spoke of was wrong. It could mean death for me and imprisonment for him. I lifted my head, met his eyes. "All the pets, we're... we're all from the pound. You choose us."

Sir Jiat ducked his head, his smile bashful. "We don't support breeders, and we feel the pets abandoned in the pound deserve more than they're given. Yes, we choose you specifically. I've always chosen older pets to take into my home."

"Where are the others?" I asked, feeling bold and brash. "Are they dead?"

"No!" Sir Jiat sighed. "I have only been part of the Movement for about a decade. It isn't long, Ewan, and if I had an abundance of pets, it would draw attention to me. There were two before you. A forty-year-old female and a twenty-six-year-old male. Both were eventually relocated to colony as soon as I could reasonably arrange it. The female was first, and then the male. You're my third, Ewan."

Disappointment rolled through me, and I didn't know why. Suddenly, I wasn't special. It hurt. "You save us. After a little while, you send us on our way. Free us," I murmured.

"It's what the Movement does." Sir Jiat reached for me, but I pulled back. "Ewan, I'm sorry. I was trying to ease you into these truths."

I swallowed, my eyes stinging. I wasn't special. His gentle touches, his reading to me, his care for me... it was what he did for all pets he took in. It left me hollowed out, tired. "May I go to bed now?" I asked, my voice thick and uneven.

Sir Jiat sat back in the water. "Of course," he murmured. "I'll be in shortly."

"I would rather sleep in the second bedroom." In my grief, my boldness remained. "If you don't mind, Master."

"You are free to sleep wherever you wish." Sir Jiat was quiet for a moment, and then said, "I will miss your heat tonight."

I rose and turned my back to him. I blinked and

two hot tears slid down my cheeks. There was nothing I could say to him. I left the bathing chamber. A glance to the bed, a bed I'd thought of as part mine since coming to Sir Jiat's, but it looked dulled and imposing now. It was where two before me had slept, and it was where all others after me would sleep. I walked from the bedroom I'd slept in for nearly five months and into the second bedroom saved for guests. It was what I was, after all. Just a guest in Sir Jiat's life. It had been such a prideful thought for me to have, expecting to be special and treasured, kept until my life wound down, but I'd been foolish. I'd fallen in love with a master who was transient. A master who was saving, not keeping, me.

In the dim room, curled up in the cold bed, I wept bitterly. My love wasn't returned, not even the slightest. It hurt in a way I'd never hurt before. I wallowed in my own misery until a light fell over my trembling body. Sir Jiat stood at the bedside, tall and pale and so beautiful it made my heart ache all the more. He held his hand out to me.

"One day, Ewan, I will take you to that colony. One day, we will leave this city behind and you'll be free, and I will be there with you," he murmured, voice warm and rumbling. "Come to bed."

I stared up into his face, those amber eyes reflecting the little bits of light in the room. There was nothing else I could do; I reached out and took his hand. He pulled me up, pressed me against his side, and led me from the cold spare room. With gentle hands, he put me under the covers of his bed, beside him instead of at his feet. He snuffed out all the lights and crawled in next to me, held me against the warmth of his body, and I wept anew.

"I thought... I wasn't special," I confessed.

Sir Jiat licked my cheek, his tongue rough against my skin. "You are special, Ewan," he whispered. "So special."

He held me as I wept. I was afraid. I was uncertain. I was hurt. I was in love with my master. I was so many things, some I didn't even know yet, but the one that followed me into the darkness of sleep was the one I wanted to be most of all: special.

Chapter Five

When dawn broke through the curtains and across my face, I rolled over, groaning softly. What I rolled into was soft fur that smelled of musk and the fine almond oil Sir Jiat liked. I cracked my eyes, peered up through my lashes. White fur and glittering amber eyes greeted me. A flush crept up my throat and face, but Sir Jiat didn't push me away. I think his arm even tightened around me. It was a safe feeling, a sense of belonging I held tightly to. All my life, I had wondered what this feeling might be like, and now I knew. But I also knew that it was a double-edged sword. Along with the belonging came the fear. Fear he would change. Fear he would cast me aside. Fear he didn't want me as I wanted him.

I couldn't let the fear rule me, though. I'd spent much of my life afraid, and I didn't want to spend what years I had left fearing. If my time with Sir Jiat was short, I wanted to revel in it as much as I could. I cleared my throat, chasing away the frog that had settled there in the night. "Master."

His paw-like hand came up to brush back my unruly hair. "I think, after all you went through last night, that you deserve a treat."

"A treat?"

Sir Jiat chuckled. "A treat, Ewan. There is a very nice groomer in the city center. Would you like to go there, be trimmed, cleaned, and made to sparkle like the diamond you are? We could then lunch at one of the nearby eateries." His hand slid across my shoulder and down my arm. "You have been kept inside so much, venturing out only when I go to one of my meetings. It's high time I showed you about."

Showed me about? I was nothing but a common mutt, nothing for my master to boast about. Or maybe I was. Sir Jiat had chosen me over all the others. He had entrusted me with his secrets. He'd told me I was special. I felt myself puff up a bit at that thought. "It sounds wonderful," I breathed, a smile coming to my lips. "I've never seen the city center."

"Then that's what we shall do today." Sir Jiat withdrew his hand, and I missed it immediately. "Hosanna should have breakfast ready for us soon, and then we will head out."

I've never eaten a meal as quickly as I did that breakfast. I was so excited about the prospect of the coming day that I couldn't slow down. I was done long before Sir Jiat, of course, and was forced to sit, impatiently squirming in my seat under his amused stare, as he calmly finished his meal. He wouldn't be rushed, and it only made my desire all the more insistent.

That excitement evaporated once we passed the boundaries of Sir Jiat's estate. I could see a few other pets being walked by their masters and mistresses, but none as old as me. I felt like an embarrassment to Sir Jiat, that he should have to be seen with such a disheveled creature at the end of his leash. Still, I kept to the brisk walking pace that Sir Jiat set for us, unwilling to be seen as difficult in addition to unkempt.

The city center was an explosion to my senses. So many new sights, sounds, and smells all around me. There were more pets than I had expected to see, more than I'd ever seen at one time, even in the pound. And with those pets were their masters. Males and females from the feline and canine lines, some chatting, some reading, all of them enjoying the unusual warmth of the day. Sir Jiat must have noticed my apprehension, because he began gently rubbing my back, instantly soothing my frazzled nerves. I focused on that touch, on the scent of my master, and the swirling chaos around me faded into something that I could handle. It was an affectionate touch, and it warmed me from the inside out.

Sir Jiat led me into the cool shadows of a shop off the main road, a little bell above the door ringing to announce us. A woman behind a bank of counters looked up from her papers and smiled at us.

"Jiat! It's a pleasure to see you again." Her icy blue eyes slid to me. She was all white, one of the canine breeds with pointy ears and fluffy fur along her body. "This must be the new pet you've kept hidden for the last season."

"Yes." Sir Jiat gave a gentle tug to my leash, and I obediently stepped forward. "As much as I have tried to keep him groomed myself, I am terrible with such things. I thought your touch would do him wonders, Kosi."

Kosi stood a little straighter at the praise. "I am the best in the city." She held out her hand, and Sir Jiat put my leash in her palm. "What is his name?"

"Ewan." Sir Jiat smiled at me. "He's obedient and sweet, the perfect pet."

S.L. Armstrong

Now it was my turn to stand a little straighter, and when Kosi led me around the counter, I went without complaint. I wanted to stay close to my master. It made me pause a moment, look over my shoulder.

"Come now, Ewan." Kosi petted my hair. "Jiat will be back for you in... hmm. I'd say two hours?" She looked up. "He needs a good bath. His hair cut. Nails manicured. Skin polished."

"Head to toe," Sir Jiat said with a chuckle. "I will return in two hours, Ewan. Be good for Kosi and I'll take you for lunch at my favorite eatery."

That promise ensured I would do anything Kosi wanted me to just so she'd give him a good report. "Yes, master," I murmured. I watched him leave the shop, and my heart began to race just as it had when Sir Jiat had first left me alone with all the other pets at his meetings. Only I couldn't look at Kosi or ask her questions. She was above me, and I bowed my head, silent and obedient.

Kosi took me behind the separation wall between the front of the shop and the actual grooming rooms. It was clean, and there were three other pets being tended to. Two were females, one male, and I only managed a quick glimpse before Kosi led me into a private room with a deep bath tub. She opened the taps, and steamy water filled the tub quickly. She added salts and oils to the water, and then turned back to me.

"You are a mess," she said, and the smile splitting her muzzle was kind. She removed my collar and leash, and then slipped my simple sandals from my feet. "At least he gives you protection for your feet." She tsked and grabbed a pitcher before shooing me into the tub. The water was so hot, the scent so rich and sweet, that I couldn't help the moan. She chuckled. "The feet of many pets are ugly, calloused and scarred. You're lucky to have such a caring master as Jiat."

I dared to say, "Yes, I am eternally grateful," just before she doused me with a pitcher full of the fragrant water. I was lucky, and I never forgot that luck. If Sir Jiat hadn't claimed me as his at the pound, I would have been long dead, put down and tossed into the lime pits or incinerator like garbage.

I was given the most thorough bath I've ever received. She even inserted a tube into my backside to wash within me as well as my flesh outside. It was an odd and uncomfortable thing that I didn't understand. Once I was clean, I was seated on a bench as Kosi took shears to my hair, and then a blade to the skin of my face, armpits, and groin. When she was done, I only had hair on my chest, arms, lower belly, and legs. She seemed to consider removing it all, but I whimpered at the idea, and she tsked as she set the blade aside.

Oiled, the shaved flesh was sensitive. As she set to trimming and buffing my toenails, I couldn't help but think of Sir Jiat smearing oil on me each day to keep my skin supple. His blade taking the hair from my body. His fingers trailing over slippery, smooth flesh. I knew it was forbidden to think such things, but I couldn't stop myself. My cock twitched shamefully, and I used my hands to cover myself from Kosi's gaze. She also filed the bottoms of my feet, oiling the skin there, and then came for my hands. I flushed brightly as I offered them to her, but she didn't look or comment on the hardness of my body. I decided then that I liked Kosi.

As a treat, while I waited for Sir Jiat, Kosi gave me a

mug of cool juice, tart and sweet on my tongue. It was truly an experience, and I couldn't stop myself from hoping that Sir Jiat would allow me this treatment frequently. I felt beautiful, my skin glowing, my hair trimmed and gleaming, and my nails buffed to a glassy shine. Kosi buckled the simple leather collar around my throat once more with a final flourish, and I could have purred with the pleasure of having that mark of ownership returned to me. But my day wasn't over and, two hours on the mark, Sir Jiat stepped through the door, making the little bell ring cheerfully. Kosi latched my leash to my collar and escorted me back to my master.

Sir Jiat's honey eyes widened, the slitted pupils contracting a moment as he took in my appearance. I felt a warmth spread over my cheeks. He was pleased. My master was pleased by my appearance, and I held my head up just a little higher as Kosi passed the leash to Sir Jiat's outstretched hand. I took my place at his side, just a step behind him, as he settled the bill with Kosi.

"You should bring him in once a month, Jiat," Kosi said as she took the thin, small sheets of silver from Sir Jiat. "He's lovely enough once he's pampered."

"Is that so?" Sir Jiat took two thin bars of copper as his change. "All right, then. A standing appointment every third Friday."

Kosi grinned. "Wonderful. I'll mark you into the schedule. Have a bright day, Jiat."

Sir Jiat led me out of the salon and onto the street once more. I walked with my head higher, and every time we were stopped by someone Sir Jiat knew, I heard murmured praise. In those moments, in the warm breeze of late afternoon, I was a prized pet, made beautiful, and my master was happy. And my day wasn't even over! There was lunch to be had, and my stomach ached to have food. I was so full of joy, I wanted to shout with it, but I was good. I was quiet. I was proud, but silent, as Sir Jiat took his seat in the outdoor cafe, and I knelt beside him. The scents around me were enticing, a promise of good food, and then Sir Jiat began to pet me. I could have died then and there, but it kept going. The petting, the pride, the joy. I didn't know how my day could become any better, any more perfect than it was now.

By the time we returned home, I was sleepy and full. All I wanted to do was curl up in the cool shadows of Sir Jiat's bed and nap until supper. Instead, he pulled me into the bedroom and told me—in that quiet, gruff voice of his—to kneel and wait for him. I was slow to go to my knees, and I swayed there, my eyelids heavy as I waited for my master. I must have dozed on my knees because one moment, Master Jiat wasn't in the room, and the next, he was crouching before me. His face with its long whiskers peered at me, an amused smile on his lips.

"Sleepy?"

I blinked slowly, unable to keep back my own smile. "Yes."

"You've had a very busy day, and your belly is full." He lifted his hands, and spread out across them was a stunning metal collar. It wasn't like the one I wore now, the one that was leather and metal, used by so many others before me. "I haven't given any of the other pets I've saved their own collar," he murmured. He reached around me and unfastened the collar at my throat. "I never cared for them beyond wanting to see them safe. Free."

My eyes met his in a bold sign of equality. Without

the collar on my throat, it was as if we were on even ground. Within these walls, in the sanctity of Sir Jiat's home, we *could* be equal, if but for a moment. "But not me?" I whispered.

"Not you. You, Ewan, have wormed your way into my life in a way no other has, and I feel you should have something all your own. Something to mark you as special." Sir Jiat slid the cool metal collar around my throat and fastened it.

I closed my eyes as the metal settled against my skin. Special. This was the second time he'd assured me I was special to him, and it made something hot and insistent rise up in my chest. I didn't know how to express the joy inside me except to fall forward and wrap my arms around his thick neck. Sir Jiat's fur was so soft, so fine, and without a thought, I pressed my lips to his. It wasn't like kissing Syra. Kissing Sir Jiat was all contradictions: soft lips and fur, sharp teeth, and a cool, damp nose. I lost myself in that moment, in those lips I'd so often wondered about, and then I came to my senses. I pulled back with a gasp, the blood pounding in my cheeks.

"I-I'm sorry," I rasped, bowing my head.

Sir Jiat lifted my chin, his honey eyes gentle, warm. "Why did you do that?"

"Today has been the best day of my life, and then you gave me your collar." My fingers found their way to the band around my throat. "I'm so happy. I didn't... didn't know how else to show it."

A rich chuckle filled the room. "Then don't be sorry," Sir Jiat said, rising from the floor. "Joy should be expressed." He ran his fingers through my hair. I closed my eyes and leaned against the muscled column of Sir Jiat's leg.

"Just remember yourself outside the walls of this home."

I nodded against his thigh. "Yes, master," I breathed. I didn't want to be parted from him, and I certainly didn't want him to lose his position in The Guard because I stupidly embraced him in public. I knew I would never jeopardize him in such a way.

"Ready for your nap?"

Again, I nodded, already drifting. The heat of his leg, the rhythmic stroking of his hand through my hair, and my still full belly made it difficult to remain alert.

Another chuckle rumbled from Sir Jiat. "Lazy Human."

Sir Jiat lifted me, and I instantly curled against the broadness of his chest. Safe. Here, I was safe. Beloved. Special. I never wanted to let that go. By the time Sir Jiat had me situated in the large bed, dreams were already clawing at me. Warmth. White fur. Honey eyes. Whiskers that tickled my lips as I opened them to welcome my master's tongue between my lips. In my dreams, I reveled in what I knew could never be.

The next meeting for Sir Jiat was almost a week after my grooming session. Sir Jiat had shaved my skin once more, oiled me, and he had even brushed my hair once I had combed his fur to gleaming. For days, I had thought the meeting at Lady Hyra's couldn't have come faster, but yet, when we arrived and I was sent out into the chilly yard with Jill, I couldn't relax into the games we played. The sunlight on my skin held no comfort with the kiss of winter approaching. The burden of my secret sapped the enjoyment from what would have been a wonderful afternoon with Jill. No matter how hard I tried to play, tried to pretend there was nothing hounding my steps, Jill wasn't a fool. She was the most observant pet I knew, though my experience with other pets was limited. After a third half-hearted attempt at competing with Jill on the metal jungle, she finally flopped down onto the grass and stared up at me.

"Do you not like me anymore?" she asked, tilting her head curiously.

"I do!" I released the too cold metal bars and collapsed beside her.

Jill pressed close to my side, and her warmth was welcome as another gust of wind bit at us. "You look really nice. Did Sir Jiat take you to the groomer?"

I nodded, my chest puffing up a little. "Yes. And Sir Jiat even shaved me before bringing me over. It was a great honor." I heard the doors open behind us, and we both sat up. Sir Jiat and Lady Hyra were standing there watching us. After a moment, Lady Hyra waved us in.

"The sun is beginning to dip. It's time to come inside. Gerta has run a hot bath for you both, and once you've warmed up, I'll have Tyne feed you both."

Sir Jiat gave me an affectionate pat and ushered me over to Gerta. The tall, broad woman was of the Lion breed, and she smiled down at us as we padded toward the lower floor bathing room. Inside, the massive tub was full, steaming, and I'd never felt colder. The moment I settled in the hot water, my fingers and toes warming slowly, I finally began to relax. I moaned softly as Gerta shut the bathing room door, leaving me alone with Jill in the bath. It was still odd to be left by myself, but I let the feeling seep out of me along with the cold.

"Are you going to tell me why you're so far away today?" Jill asked as she picked up the bar of soap and set to scrubbing the grass and dirt from me.

I blushed, ducking my head shyly. Could I tell her? Or would she tell Lady Hyra, who would then tell The Guard? I didn't want to risk Sir Jiat, but the need to confide in *someone* boiled inside me. Finally, I murmured, "I kissed Sir Jiat." At her puzzled look, I clarified. "I pressed my lips to his. It was wonderful and everything I had thought it might be."

"You've only kissed him?"

"Yes." I nodded, glancing down at the suds in the water. "Though... I ache for more." As much as I liked feeling what I felt for Sir Jiat, it also brought me shame. It was forbidden. Pets were never supposed to lust for their masters, and before now, I never had. But Sir Jiat... his touch... his voice... his gaze...

Jill laughed softly. "I understand."

I frowned. "Do you?"

As she rinsed my body, Jill nodded. "I do. Lady Hyra and I have been more than mistress and pet since my sixteenth year." Jill was now in her twenty-seventh year, so I was shocked to hear that Lady Hyra had been her mate for the last eleven years. Eleven years! "We're careful, but..." Jill smiled. "I love her, and she loves me."

I stared at her with my mouth agape. Jill and Lady Hyra. It explained why Lady Hyra's home wasn't exactly catering to a pet's needs. In these walls, Jill wasn't a possession. Jill was a lover. A mate. The truth rocked me. Here was a pet who was living the fantasy I had created in my own head! It *was* possible. It was dangerous. It was against the law. But it was *possible*. That possibility was all I needed.

"So cheer up." Jill grinned at me and pressed her

fingers to my chin, closing my mouth. "If you love Sir Jiat, and if he loves you in return, a life together is real. It takes thought, and it means understanding the difference between your relationship inside his home—and homes like Hyra's—and your relationship in the city, or when those not of the Movement are around." A shadow passed through Jill's gaze. "It can hurt in the beginning, not being able to share your love with the world and be as if we were of their race, too, but the pain is worth it. Her touches to my flesh, her soft words, her *love* for me... it's worth it."

I tilted my head, chewing on the words as Jill washed herself. To love Sir Jiat more than I did, I would have to sacrifice. Didn't I sacrifice already? How much would truly change if I knew his body as I had known Syra's? I chewed at my lip until I winced and tasted blood. The heart of the matter was not whether or not *I* was willing to risk myself, but if Sir Jiat was willing to risk all he had: a home, a position in The Guard, a place in society. He had so much more than I did to lose, and that couldn't make taking me into his bed as a lover very tempting. I deflated a little in the tub, huddling in on myself. I wanted him, and though he had told me I was special, just how special was I? Was I special enough to risk everything for?

Chapter Six

My knees hurt. Winter had come, and the combination of the cold weather and the icy, bare floor beneath me left me gritting my teeth. Sir Jiat sat in a chair, turning the pages of some sort of pamphlet the pound left out on the tables in the receiving room. I wanted to shift, stretch my back, but I wasn't allowed. My collar was tight, the lead attached to it taut to keep my back slightly bowed. It was the proper posture for a pet, but it was a posture I hadn't been forced into for any length of time over the last six months. Sir Jiat liked me relaxed, comfortable, but this situation was neither. My six month check in. This was when a master could return his adopted pet for whatever reason. Despite Sir Jiat's assurances before we'd left the house, fear coiled through me. The smell of the pound, the sterile colors, the harsh edges of everything... I wanted to curl against Sir Jiat, beg him to protect me, keep me. This place was hell, and my next step if I was returned yet again was the back room where pets met their end to save a little coin for the city.

I shook myself. No. Sir Jiat had no intention of returning me. He didn't. And he wouldn't lie to me. Never had he lied to me. We were here merely to check in, and then we would go home and this would be forever behind me. I took a deep breath and let it out slowly. Of course, Sir Jiat would be in just as much trouble as me if he did return me. The things I knew were enough to condemn him and others right alongside me. No, if Jiat ever tired of me, he would have no choice but to dispatch me himself in order to protect his secrets. Not a comforting thought, that, but then, this wasn't a comforting place.

Finally, we were called back into the examination room. Sir Jiat removed my collar and helped me to step up onto the cold metal table. Several more minutes passed before the shelter's doctor came in. Dr. Tiwan's coat was white, whiter even than the sterile, blank walls of this place, which only made his green eyes glow the brighter. Tiwan had been working at the shelter the first time I arrived, and it seemed that he'd be here long after I never had to fear returning.

"Back again, are we, Ewan?" Tiwan asked, not waiting for an answer. "How has he been for you, Sir Jiat? I did warn you when you first adopted him that he was a bit precocious."

Jiat nodded. "You did, but I have to say, it was totally unnecessary. Ewan has been exemplary in my care."

"A reflection, no doubt, of your exceptional skills as a trainer. As I've always said, Humans do possess a fair amount of intelligence and can learn even complex tasks, but left to their own devices, they never survive for long. The dull teeth, spindly, unclawed fingers, and lack of even the barest coat make them completely unsuitable for life on their own. Fortunately, there are individuals like you who are willing to overlook that and take the poor things in."

"Of course." Sir Jiat was annoyed; I could tell by the way his paws were flexing by his sides and how the tip of his tail twitched. He gestured in my direction. "Would you mind, Tiwan? I'm afraid I do have other matters that require my attention today."

Tiwan looked over at me and seemed to remember I was in the room. "Oh! Yes, certainly. I know how hectic the life of a Guard can be." He started checking me over for any cuts or scrapes that might require attention. Unfortunately, he continued speaking the entire time. "It's worse for mutts like this one, of course. A competent breeder can weed out things like aggression or stupidity. Ones like this, born out in the wild... well, they don't have that benefit. It's almost impossible to fully tame them. You never know when they might do something... unexpected."

On that last word, Tiwan pinched my side, hard. I yelped and jerked away before I could stop myself. I covered my mouth with my hand, looking guiltily toward Sir Jiat. My lovely owner, though, merely smiled at me and nodded to tell me that I'd done nothing wrong.

"I take the welfare of my pets very seriously," Sir Jiat stated flatly. "I would appreciate it if you didn't molest them any more than strictly necessary to complete your examination." Sir Jiat puffed himself up slightly, emphasizing the height advantage he had over Tiwan.

Tiwan visibly flinched, and I allowed myself a small, internal moment of perverse glee. "Of course. Apologies, Sir Jiat. So, am I to take this to mean that you are not intending to return Ewen to us today?"

"Not today, not ever."

I nearly fainted at the conviction in those words. I started thinking back over the conversation with Jill and her relationship with Lady Hyra. Up to now, I had imagined that Sir Jiat and I could have that kind of love with one another, but I had never seriously thought that it could happen. Not until that moment, until I heard those words from him, spoken with such certainty. It seemed he was almost daring Tiwan to challenge him. I felt my cheeks grow hot, and my cock stirred between my legs and began to harden. I clenched my eyes shut and forced it to stop. I couldn't risk giving anything away here.

Tiwan seemed not to notice, thankfully, and he finished his examination of me with no further commentary on my inferiority. No, he had to start rambling about purebreeds. Purebreeds, the ones everyone vied to buy. The expensive, pampered pets whose bloodlines were cherished, cultivated, and coveted. I understood why most of Sir Jiat's companions chose to adopt mutts, as purebreeds weren't in the precarious positions most mutts were. Our lives were cheap. We were *disposable*. Once we were too old, once the shine was gone and the kittens and puppies grew out of their love for us... Our love didn't matter. Our devotion was only worthy while we were young and pretty. There was a reason I never saw *old* mutts. We either came here, to the back room, or we had 'accidents'. Easily replaced at the feet of the family we served.

"Did you hear about Mistress Lyl's pet? What was its name?" Tiwan asked as he poked and prodded me, checked to make sure Sir Jiat hadn't been mistreating me. It was only cursory; if he had found bruises on me, obvious signs of abuse, I don't think he would have confiscated me.

Sir Jiat's eyes narrowed a little. "*His* name was Jac, and yes, I have heard. It's a sad thing when one's pet meets their end. I sent my condolences this morning."

Who was Mistress Lyl? And who was Jac? I looked to Sir Jiat, but he shook his head almost imperceptibly. If I was to know who they were, this was not the place I would be told.

Tiwan tsked, his whiskers twitching. "I saw to the poor boy last night and sent my report to the Guardhouse. I believe Sir Vais was overseeing the case. The third mutt to be lost this month. I would say it's a shame, but—"

"Yes, your opinion of mutts is quite clear," Sir Jiat snapped, his ears pressing back. "If we are through here?"

Tiwan nodded, making notes on some papers across the room. "I will close out your file, Sir Jiat." He turned back to us and smiled, showing his sharp teeth. "It was a pleasure seeing you again, and I wish you luck with your pet."

Sir Jiat slid the collar around my neck once more, gave my leash a sharp tug, and I slid off the table, keeping my back as straight as possible. He led me through the rooms, but I didn't notice anything around me beyond how my joints ached. The bitter wind awaited me, and I wasn't looking forward to the walk home. My feet were protected by my precious sandals, but my body was bare to the winter elements. The walk here had been terrible, and I only realized I was whining when Sir Jiat gave my leash another tug. I looked up at him, a fine tremble moving through me.

"Enough, Ewan," Sir Jiat said, his tone sharp. I didn't like that tone. For me, it was worse than a whip's strike.

I lowered my eyes again as Sir Jiat opened the door, the wind swirling around me, the soft kiss of ice dancing over my skin. Almost instantly, my teeth began to chatter. I followed Sir Jiat to the curb, and a third tug to my leash brought my eyes up once more to see the protected cab of a carriage waiting for us. The door opened, and Lady Hyra smiled out at us, Jill seated on a plush pillow at Lady Hyra's feet. Sir Jiat stepped inside and sat opposite Lady Hyra, and I joined him, kneeling on the second, empty pillow by his feet. The door shut, and I was blissfully warm, protected.

Sir Jiat's hand combed through my hair, encouraging me to lean against his furry knee. I closed my eyes, smiling as I did just that. The carriage jerked forward, and we were on our way home.

"Jac is safe?" Sir Jiat asked.

"Yes." Lady Hyra. Her voice was quiet, subdued. "His leg is broken, but our runner did report back that he is safe in the colony. Poor Lyl. She wasn't quite ready to let Jac go, but I think they were beginning to draw attention."

Sir Jiat grunted, his claws gently scratching at my scalp. "You must be careful, too. I do not want anyone to rip Jill away from you. Not until you are ready to go to the colony with her."

Jac. Another pet. Another mutt who had fallen in love with his mistress. Another pet sent to this colony. I nuzzled Sir Jiat's knee, not bothering to open my eyes. I was content. No one was going to take me from Sir Jiat, and though I loved him—and I thought he loved me—I didn't think I could have what Jill had. I didn't want to hope, though Sir Jiat's words still echoed in my mind, tempting me.

You are special, Ewan.
Maybe... just maybe...
I hoped.

Once we were home, I was rushed into the bathing room, where Hosanna had already drawn a steaming bath. Sir Jiat removed my leash but left the fine collar around my throat.

"Into the tub," Sir Jiat ordered, and I happily complied.

I couldn't help but moan. Even in the safety of the carriage, there had been a bit of a draft. My toes were so very cold, and my joints still ached. The hot water lapped at my body, chased away the worst of the chill. When I opened my eyes after settling into the tub, Sir Jiat was gazing down at me. There was an odd look to his amber eyes, something curious and uncertain. I didn't understand it, but still, my cheeks tinted red. I could feel them throb with the blush.

"I am truly yours, then?" I asked, my voice soft in the echoing room.

Sir Jiat gave a small nod. "Yes," he murmured, and the word sounded almost like a purr. By the stars, I wanted to hear him purr. I wanted to *feel* his purr, know that my hands, my body, made him purr. "No more trips to the pound. You belong to me."

I shuddered, and he had to have seen it. It made the water ripple. "Good," I breathed. I didn't want to belong to anyone else, not even the High Lord himself.

After another moment of watching me, Sir Jiat grabbed a bar of soap and a sponge. He knelt beside the tub and began to wash me. I didn't need to be washed. Warmed, yes, but not washed. Hosanna had bathed me this morning before breakfast in preparation for the trip to see Dr. Tiwan. So, why was Sir Jiat washing me now? He had to have given Hosanna the order to wash me. He began with my back, and I moaned again, letting my head fall forward. Whether I'd been washed that morning or not, I loved feeling Sir Jiat's hands on me. It didn't take long before his paw replaced the sponge, the bare pads soaped and slick over my wet skin. That intimate touch did things to me I was both ashamed of and desperate to experience.

His hand moved along my chest as I lay back against the slanted side of the tub, my legs stretched out in front of me. The gentle slosh of water and my own breathing were the only sounds as Sir Jiat's fingers slid over my nipples. I was hard. There was no hiding it. He made me want in ways I didn't understand, but I didn't care. He was touching me under the thin guise of washing. Still, I knew he was touching me because he *wanted* to. It was there for me to feel as his paw slid down my stomach, over a hip. The want I felt was inside him, too, but as his fingers brushed just below my navel and I held my breath, I didn't know if he would act on our mutual want.

There was a moment of stillness, of decision, and then Sir Jiat withdrew, grabbing a towel and wiping his hands as he stood up. There was a hardness hidden by his loincloth, something more to tempt my fevered dreams with. He cleared his throat. "Finish washing," he ordered, voice so deep and gruff. "We will have supper, and then I shall read to you before bed."

"Yes, Master," I murmured, and I didn't recognize my own voice, the thickness to it.

He left me alone in the hot, soapy water with need pounding between my legs. Doubt began to creep into my thoughts. No one would have seen us share pleasure. The obvious hardness of my cock should have shown how much I *wanted* to share pleasure with him. But... but maybe he didn't really want that. Had I imagined the glow of his eyes when he'd looked at me? Had his touch been clinical and I'd only read into it what my fantasy demanded? Oh, I didn't know! I frowned at the soapy water, my brow furrowed as confusion and uncertainty raged through me alongside my desire.

I washed, though I didn't pay much attention as I did so. I dried myself, oiled my flesh, and combed my hair. By the time I presented myself for supper, my cock had relaxed once more, though I didn't look up from my plate. I still found it so strange to sit at a table, in a chair, and eat with knife and spoon. Eating was mechanical, and the sounds of utensils on plates, the clink of glasses, was the only sound between us at the table. Sir Jiat didn't speak to me as he usually did, and I truly began to worry. Had I ruined something by moaning? By growing firm at his touch? Moon and sun, I hope I hadn't. I didn't want to be sent to that colony without him.

I brushed his fur in silence back in the master bedroom. Our eyes didn't meet. I relished touching him, and when his coat gleamed, he turned the lamps down and nodded to the bed. I climbed up and settled under the covers on my side of the bed, my head cradled by the soft, down-stuffed pillow. Such a luxury. I drank in the sight of him as he made himself comfortable, resting his glasses on his nose before opening the book he'd been reading to me for the last two weeks. It was a wild adventure where a noble from the Cougars seeks to free and wed a captured maid from the clutches of an evil Jackal witch. It was a lavish story with swords and foul words and love. His voice was low, soothing, and I couldn't help but inch closer and closer as he turned the page. As Gref, the Cougar, battled Slehb the Witch, I pressed my body flush to his hip and leg. Even with the heath lit and the windows shuttered against he first snows of winter, there was a slight damp chill in the home. Sir Jiat was hot, warming me, and though he paused as I nuzzled his side, he didn't push me away. He resumed the story, and I remained pressed close, his scent strong in my nose as I slowly drifted into desire filled dreams.

Chapter Seven

A gentle combing of my hair woke me the following morning, making my scalp tingle. It took a moment for my eyes to cooperate, but when they opened, my vision was filled with the sight of Sir Jiat hovering over me. His fingers were carding through my hair over and over, slowly and tenderly. I smiled, closed my eyes, and stretched, my body shaking the last bits of sleep as I yawned. When I settled once more and looked up at him again, I saw something in his eyes I hadn't seen before. Something hot, a flickering in the honeyed depths of his eyes that made my morning need tighten low in my body. I swallowed and licked my lips as I felt heat move over my cheeks. Something needed to be said, done, but I didn't know what, and so I merely remained on my back staring up at him, uncertainty painted on my face.

Sir Jiat continued to pet me, but his fingers began to trail along my neck, shoulder. My pulse would jump every time the rough pad of his finger would stroke over my throat. My cock seemed to move with the force of my heartbeat under the blankets, and I was terrified he would look down, see the bedclothes tented over my groin. When I thought I couldn't take any more of this simple intimacy, my master finally spoke.

"I have sent Hosanna and Werrs away today. They will not return until tomorrow morning." Sir Jiat's eyes shifted, slid down along the length of my body. "I know what it is you want. I even think I know what it is you feel."

The words burned in my throat, demanded to be given voice. "I love you," I whispered. "I know I love you. Not as master. You are a good master, but..."

Sir Jiat smiled. "But?"

"But you are more than master." The heat of my cheeks intensified. "You are special."

His eyes softened as he gazed at me, and his large hand smoothed over my chest. "As are you, Ewan. So very, very special. No Human has captured my heart as you have. Without trying, you tempt me to turn away from this life I have so carefully built. Risk it all to press my lips to yours. My body to yours."

"Will you?" I was so bold! I was asking him to throw everything away and love me. I couldn't believe the words had passed my lips.

Sir Jiat stared into my eyes for what felt like an eternity, and then he nodded once, slowly. "Yes," he murmured gruffly. He dipped down, and my heart seemed to stop in my chest as his muzzle opened and his broad, rough tongue slid out and lapped over my parted lips. It wasn't how a Human kissed, but I didn't care. It was how Sir Jiat kissed me, the first kiss, and I would never forget the feeling of the rough muscle, the slight dryness, or the sweetness of his breath. He must have brushed his teeth after sending Hosanna and Werrs away, and something warm unfurled inside me. Sir Jiat had planned this moment with me.

He licked at my lips over and over, taking his time,

and when my lips tingled from the roughness of his tongue, he dipped inside to taste me. Uncertain, nervous, I lifted my hands and slid them down his back, through his soft, pale fur. The moan he made rumbled between our mouths, and I heard myself whine. Oh, oh, by the moon and stars, I was practically shaking with my arousal. I brought my hands up to cup his face, and I let my fingers slide up to caress his ears as I began to kiss first one side, and the other, of Sir Jiat's muzzle. Little movements of my lips and tongue against his mouth, my hands exploring every inch of him they could reach.

When Sir Jiat tilted his head back, and my lips began to press along the fur and flesh there, I felt it. The purr. The purr that became louder, deeper, the longer my mouth teased his neck. What arousal coursed through me soon became suffocating, and I whined as I bit at the rumbling beneath my lips. "Please," I panted, not knowing what it was I was asking him for. I put myself in his hands, hoping wildly that Sir Jiat knew what I simply did not.

"It's all right," Sir Jiat purred near my ear.

He pulled the bedclothes from my body and shoved them down to the foot of the bed. Though he'd seen me naked daily, and aroused on a few occasions, the way he looked at me now made me think he was truly seeing me for the first time. I flushed again, and my hands itched to cover my cock. His broad hands smoothed down my chest, his sharp claws pricking at my nipples. My nipples drew up tight as pleasure sizzled along my nerves. I gasped and my hips shifted, arched just a little. A wicked smile split Sir Jiat's muzzle, and he leaned down and began to torture my nipples with little sandpapery licks. How my head spun!

I lost all sense of time, of myself, as he nipped and

licked at me, from my neck to my nipples, from nipple to navel. My stomach jumped each time his tongue delved into that little indent, and when I laughed, he grinned up at me. Then, he inched down just a bit more, and his hot, moist breath danced over my hot cock. I moaned... or maybe I mewled, I don't know. Whatever sound left my throat, Sir Jiat loved. His purr became deafening just before he drew his tongue from my balls up to the tip of my cock. It was a languid, possessive touch, a sensation that left my balls aching. Without a thought, I spread my legs wide, offered all my most sensitive parts up to him to feast upon. I trusted my master with my heart and body, and I was instantly rewarded.

Sir Jiat lapped at my sac, my thighs, my cock. If I bared it to him, he took it as his. He scent-marked each of my thighs, a soft growl in his throat as he did it. "Mine," he told me, and then his cool nose nudged at the base of my cock. I was trembling, aching, my hips arching up eagerly into every touch. "I want to taste you at your source," he murmured, and then he focused on the tip of my cock. He drew the skin back, exposed that sensitive head, and then his tongue slid over my slit.

The strangled, high-pitched cry that I uttered shocked even me. I thought of nothing but that rasp of tongue over the engorged tip, again and again, until I squeezed my eyes shut and bucked. I shouted as climax seared through my brain, wracked my body, and I spilled my seed against Jiat's tongue. My life, I knew, would never again be the same, and I wept as I shivered in the aftermath.

Jiat's arms encircled me, and he nosed my cheek, lapped at the tears, and I turned into him, burying my face against his throat. He held me until the tears stopped, until my body had stilled, his hands always petting, soothing me. I lifted my face so I could look up at him. "I've never felt like that before," I admitted. "Not even when you took me to Syra."

"It is different when you love and care for the one in your bed." Jiat brushed back the hair from my face. "I've rarely let myself love another. The very nature of what I do for Humans means secrecy and betrayal. I have to protect myself and whatever pet I have taken in, and that can be lonely."

"But I'm different."

Jiat chuckled, his hand gliding down my side, over my hip, to rest on my thigh. "You, Ewan, are *very* different. I've fallen in love with you."

I couldn't help the smile that graced my face. He'd said it. He loved me. I couldn't help but pounce on him, kiss his muzzle and neck and shoulders. "I love you, too," I whispered over his heart. I let my hands wander, touch and learn his body. He was so strong, muscled and thick in so many places. My guard. My protector. Jiat moaned as I circled his nipples with my fingers. This was easy. I mimicked what he had done, scratching my nails over the tight buds. I even pinched them, and he growled, his tail flicking impatiently on the bed. I smiled, bent my head, and drew one between my lips, suckling and licking. The sounds he made! What desire had drained from me during my release surged back, more vicious and demanding than ever. I was hard against his hip, and I could feel him against mine. Slippery. Long. So very, very hot. But as I kissed and licked and nipped over his chest and down his sculpted stomach, I didn't know what to do. Not really. Not beyond licking at him as he had at me.

Was that all there was? Licking? Biting? Touching? I glanced up at him as I straddled his thighs. "I... I don't know..."

Jiat's words were warm, soft. "Touch me," he murmured. He took my hand in his and pressed my palm to the slick heat of his cock.

I looked down and stared. Jiat was shaped oddly. Well, compared to my own cock. For one, it jutted out of a furry pouch, and his balls were covered in his white fur, too. It was strange, but he said I could touch, and so I did. I ran my finger around that area where his bare cock met that furred sheath. Jiat moaned, and a rush of power filled me. I could make him as weak as he made me, and the realization was intoxicating. I traced upward, over the very slick, smooth, pink flesh, and when I came close to the elegantly tapered tip, the texture changed. I rubbed there, just under the head of him, feeling firm, slightly stiff barbs. They weren't prickly or scratchy, but they were so odd! I leaned down and, yes, decorating along the top third of Jiat's cock, just under the head, were soft, pliable barbs of flesh!

My eyes met his, and I saw amusement mingling with his arousal. "You have little bumps!"

"The Felines do." Jiat chuckled. "It pleasures the females. Helps us with conception. Do you not like them?"

I shook my head, smiling. "I love them. I love learning about this part of you." I traced up again, and now I played with the tip of him. Where I was rounded and blunt, he was elongated and pointed. And in the slit there at the peak, beads of slippery, clear fluid gathered. I swiped my finger through the fluid and brought it to my lips, blushing as Jiat watched me. It was musky, thick on my tongue, but not unpleasant. I smiled at him. "So slick," I whispered.

"Do you like it?"

I nodded. "Yes."

"Will you press your lips to me? Lick and suck at me?"

Jiat didn't order me about, he asked. Most of my life, I'd been forced to always say yes, the option of 'no' never being real. But it was real here. I could say no, and nothing would come of it. But I didn't *want* to say no. Instead, I leaned in and drew my tongue over him. I had no basis for comparison, no lover in my past that I could draw experience from. Part of me was glad for that.

When I reached the tip of him, I suckled, licked, and his groans and growls only encouraged me. I threw myself into worshipping Jiat's cock with my mouth. I couldn't suck him too far into my mouth, but I used my hands to touch every inch my mouth couldn't. I didn't give up, even when those clear fluids seemed to become stronger in flavor. It was part of Jiat, and the mewls and moans told me what I did, Jiat liked. His claws scratched at my scalp a little, and then tangled in my hair. Jiat's hips began to rise and fall, shift from side to side, and then he yowled. His cock jerked in my hand, and my mouth flooded with his seed. I was shocked, unprepared—though I shouldn't have been—and I wasn't as graceful or skilled as Jiat. I made a mess of him and myself, and my embarrassment burned red from my chest to the very tip of my ears. I didn't want to look up because I didn't want to be faced with his disappointment in me.

"Ewan."

Slowly, I met his eyes, but there was only lazy satisfaction to be read in them. "Yes?"

Jiat was purring, drawing me up the length of him,

and then he began to lick at my mouth and chin, cleaning up the mess I'd made. "Mmm... that was..." He sighed, a grin on his face. "That was wonderful."

I smiled, too, relaxing against him. "I was messy."

"That will lessen with practice." His eyes sparkled. "You would like to practice, right?"

Now I laughed, nuzzling his shoulder. "Yes. Lots of practice."

"Well, we have all day and night together, no interruptions. I will make us food, and after we've eaten..." Jiat licked at my throat. "I want to show you a new pleasure."

I shivered in his arms, already impatient to learn this new pleasure of his. But he eased me back, kissed me again, and then rose, padding off into the house. I could hear sounds in the kitchen, and then the scent of meat cooking. I grinned up at the ceiling, my stomach rumbling and my limbs weak. This, I decided, was the best day of my life.

I'd fallen asleep after eating the meal Jiat had brought me. A full belly, a sunbeam, and the quiet of the house had made it impossible for me to keep my eyes open. Curled up against the naked, solid form of my lover, I'd let sleep take me. No nightmares haunted my sleep, and I don't remember if I dreamed. It was peaceful. My mind at rest, and Jiat's hand petting me as he read, I napped. I didn't budge until I heard his voice, felt his whiskers teasing my shoulder. I moaned and shifted against the bed, my half-hard cock pressed to the mattress. His rough tongue lapped down my spine, and I sighed.

"Master," I breathed.

"No," Jiat said gently. "Jiat. Please, my name, Ewan..."

Jiat's damp, cool nose brushed over the swell of my ass, and I shivered. "Jiat." I looked over my shoulder and down at him as he urged me to spread my legs. "What are you doing?"

"I told you, after we ate, I was going to show you something new. Something pleasurable." Jiat's hands cupped each of my ass cheeks and spread me open.

I blushed brightly as he exposed my hole. "W-What pleasure c-can be had *there*?"

Jiat chuckled. "I think you might be surprised." He dipped his head, and a moment later, I felt his broad, rough tongue sliding between my cheeks.

I shuddered as the tingling sensation washed over me. Jiat continued to lick, drawing his tongue from the top of my hole all the way down until it brushed against my balls. My cock responded instantly, and my breath came out in ragged sighs. He was right; I was surprised by how good it felt. I wanted to tell him, but I couldn't pull my wits together enough to form the words. I think I may have moaned, "More," at some point.

What that 'more' was, I didn't know. But I trusted Jiat. He had to know. After a while, Jiat sat back and reached for the bedside table. I watched with hazy eyes as he lifted a bottle of amber oil from the drawer. I hadn't seen that bottle before, and when he lifted the cork, the scent of milky almonds filled the room. Closing my eyes, I inhaled deeply and smiled. I liked that smell. It brought to mind images of safety and motherhood. I wondered briefly if my mother had used almond oil, but then Jiat drizzled the oil over the cleft of my ass and any thought of that vague memory flew apart. I moaned and arched my back a little, exposing more of my hidden places to Jiat. He rubbed his broad finger against my hole, smearing the oil, but he never pressed inward, that claw at the tip both dangerous and deadly.

"You'll need to help me," Jiat murmured behind me. "I've never been intimate with a Human, and my hands are not fit to do what must be done before we join."

My heart pounded in my ears as I swallowed against my dry throat. I lifted my head to glance behind me at Jiat, and I was stunned by his beauty. Broad, tall, his white fur and honey eyes, and when I let my eyes drift lower, I saw his cock again. It stood proud, slick and dusky in color. I licked my lips and nodded. "What must I do?" I rasped.

Jiat took my hand and poured some of the almond oil onto my three middle fingers, and I watched as drops fell to the bed. "You will need to ease first one finger inside your body, and then a second. I want you to push in and out for a minute, just to oil yourself thoroughly."

"A-All right." My cheeks were a brilliant red as I reached back and pressed my finger to my hole. I'd never touched myself like this before, and to do so with Jiat's eyes focused on me... I licked my lips and pushed in. The sensation was strange, but the oil made it easy, and it didn't take much for me to slide in to my knuckle. Jiat moaned then, and my eyes jerked up to find him staring at where my finger had disappeared. "Like this?" I asked, my voice faint, breathless as need and embarrassment coiled through me.

"Yes," Jiat moaned as I pulled my finger out, and then pushed it back in. "Just like that."

Suddenly, I didn't feel as embarrassed, as vulnerable. There was power in what I did. Maybe not power against the city as a whole, but power in this room. Here. Now. That power filled me, and I eased my middle finger in alongside the other, and this time, it pulled a groan from me. There was an edge of pain now, something sharp dancing at the edge of whatever ledge I was about to leap from.

"The discomfort is normal. Just try to ease yourself open so you're well oiled." Jiat's words were encouraging, but there was something more under his words, something he wasn't saying. The worry was there and gone just as quickly, though, as the slight pain fizzled out. The more I moved my fingers, the easier it seemed to get. I was just getting into a rhythm when a gentle touch to my arm made me pause.

"Enough," Jiat breathed, and his voice... by the stars, his *voice*. It was barely more than a growl, and it dripped with things I could barely understand. "Lean over with your hands firmly on the bed." My heart raced as I did as he said, my hands pressed to the bed. I felt him move behind me, the heat of him so close now.

I closed my eyes, and the slick sounds of oil and hand and cock filled my senses. I shuddered, fear gripping me as Jiat pressed the pointed tip of him against my hole. My hole twitched as Jiat pushed against it, demanded my body let him inside. His hands were hot and strong on my hips, holding me still, and the more of him that slid within, the louder the whine in my throat became. How large was he? How long? My hands twisted in the sheets, and I gritted my teeth, panting as the slight discomfort became a stinging burn... and then became *painful*. "J-Jiat—"

Jiat's breath was hot against my neck. "I know," he growled, "how difficult it can be the first time. But you must breathe through it."

Breathe through it? How was I supposed to breathe through being torn in half by his cock? I bowed my head to the bed, breathing fast and shallow, my head swimming. "It hurts."

"I know, love, I know." Jiat didn't stop, though. He kept pushing in, and with every inch, I swore I couldn't take any more. My head swam, and my vision darkened on the edges when he stopped moving. "There," he purred, the word trilling beautifully. "You have all of me inside you, Ewan. Gods, you grip me like nothing I've felt before!"

I couldn't help but whimper. I was unbelievably full. I wanted to bear down. His hands left my hips and began to stroke up and down my sides, my back. The tenderness in the touch pulled the sob from my throat. Jiat was inside me. *Inside me.* The thing I couldn't have even fantasized about was happening, and I was terrified, overjoyed, and desire pounded through me with the rhythm of my heart.

Then, Jiat moved. Just the slightest shift within. Back and in. After another moment, he did it again, just as slight. The third time, he pulled back a little more, and then rolled his hips forward, thrusting so deeply inside me. Those barbs at the end of him did drag inside me, but it wasn't painful like I'd thought it would be. It was texture. They rubbed against my walls, tickled at my senses inside, and when he finally almost pulled out only to press back inside, I cried out as burning fullness morphed into tingling pleasure. Oh, gods of the stars, my cock leaked beneath me, jerking each time Jiat thrust inward.

"Yes," Jiat hissed, his nails scratching lightly down my back and over my ass. "Move with me, Ewan. Revel in our shared pleasure."

How could I deny him? Deny myself? Outside our room, it would be a death sentence, but here, in this bed he'd shared with me for months, it was sacred. I lifted my head and moaned, the sound lewd, rumbling, and when Jiat thrust in this time, I pushed back. He touched me so deeply, in places I never imagined I could find pleasure, and I sang my joy to the sun-washed ceiling. Jiat never sped up, never fucked me as I'd seen some of the male cats take females. In every thrust was respect, love, care. I felt it in his hands, in his breath on my skin, in the way his cock laid claim to my body.

Time ceased to have meaning to me. Jiat's rough tongue slid over my sweaty back. His teeth left little marks on my shoulders. My toes curled, and my cock ached to be touched. I wanted to feel it all explode through my mind again with Jiat buried within, but Jiat drew it out. He let it build inside us until I thought I'd go mad with want. When his large paw finally wrapped around my cock, I knew I was at the edge, hanging on by only my fingertips, and I trembled, gasped, shook my head. "Oh! Oh, stars above!"

And still, his touch was tender, slow, his thrusts never hurried, his voice never demanding. My release came in its time, a rush of heat and searing pleasure that bordered on pain. I choked on my scream, and Jiat seemed to grow so much larger within me. I rippled around him, clutched at him as my seed painted our bed in pearly ribbons. There was nothing in my life—in all my days—that I could compare that moment to, and I knew I never wanted to give Jiat up. I loved him as master, as friend, as lover, and my life would lose so much if his light left it.

My arms gave out from under me, and my chest fell to the mattress. I twitched with the aftershocks, and Jiat's growl behind me brought a new, plaintive moan from the depths of me. Jiat was still moving inside me, and there was no resistance. My body welcomed him deeper, my cock still cradled in his hand, and those barbs rubbed at all the right places. I relaxed, let my body move with him, in his deep, slow rhythm, and when his claws pricked at my hips, I was ready. I closed my eyes and focused, wanting to commit that moment to my memory forever. Jiat's movements hitched, stuttered, and then he thrust as deep as he could and yowled.

Unbelievable heat rushed into me, coating those hidden parts of me. The scent of his musk grew stronger as he shifted back and forth, rubbing against my slick walls, dragging out our shared pleasure. It was so unique, so intense, and I wanted to know it all over again. I turned my head when he stilled inside me and opened my eyes. Jiat's eyes were closed, his chest heaving, and the grin that split his muzzle was one of sated, smug happiness. I couldn't help but smile, too.

Jiat's hands resumed stroking up and down my back and sides, and his purr... his purr was so beautiful and loud. It rumbled through the room, echoed in my ears, and I was happy. It was *my* happiness, and I didn't want to let it go. I whimpered when Jiat sat back, his cock leaving me with a wet sound.

"Shh," Jiat murmured. He leaned in, his tongue snaking between my cheeks again, and his broad tongue licked over my used hole. I gasped and squirmed, the flesh tender and hypersensitive, but he didn't stop. He cleaned me, lick by lick, and then eased me over onto my side so he could gather me into his arms. I went willingly, my body limp, my eyes heavy. He brushed our lips together as he smoothed back my hair. "You are the most precious creature in my life."

I looked up at him, into his eyes. "I love you," I breathed.

Jiat smiled. "As I love you."

Those words complicated everything between us as much as they simplified it. I closed my eyes and cuddled close, listening to his purr rumble under my ear. There was no hope for me to remain awake, and I fell into a deep, dreamless sleep within moments, all the places within me silent.

S.L. Armstrong

Chapter Eight

I woke to the sound of hushed voices. I cracked by eyes only enough to see the bedroom door open a crack, and through that crack, I could hear Jiat and Hosanna speaking. I immediately closed my eyes again, and I didn't move. Hosanna's voice carried best, higher and clearer than Jiat's, and she was very clearly upset.

"I worried this very thing would happen. I told you. I saw how you looked at him, how he looked at you, and I *said—*"

Jiat's voice rumbled. "I will be very careful. I know what I'm doing, and as long we're discreet..."

Hosanna huffed. "Discreet. If you're discovered..." She was quiet for a moment. "Abomination, Jiat. That's the charge. And the only penalty is *death*. The High Council likes sending clear messages that mating with pets is forbidden, and they will make an example of you. One of the *Guard* rutting with a mutt?"

"Hosanna." Jiat's voice had an edge to it I'd never heard before. "This is not some *mutt*. Have more respect than that. This is Ewan."

"Forgive me." Hosanna sighed, and I saw her shadow shift outside the door. "I simply worry. You're my friend, someone dear, and I worry."

Jiat moved out from my line of sight, and I heard rustling. I wondered if he was kissing her... touching her... reassuring her. How could a Human—who he wasn't even allowed to openly love as an equal—compare to another of his kind? The stab of jealousy made my chest ache, and I turned in the bed so I lay on my back. My eyes stung with tears as I imagined all the things going on just outside the door.

After a moment, the door swung open again and in stepped Jiat, a tray in his hands. I looked over in time to see Hosanna close the door behind him. Jiat paused halfway to the bed, cocking his head. "Why are you weeping?"

I shook my head. I didn't want to say why. Saying it out loud made me feel foolish, childish.

Jiat came to the bedside and set the tray on the mattress at my feet before climbing up beside me. "Now, none of that. We must always speak when upset. It helps to ease a heavy heart. Do you still hurt from yesterday?"

"Just a little," I admitted, my backside throbbing only if I moved too quickly and carelessly.

"Then why the tears?"

I couldn't look at him. "I... heard you talking to Hosanna. And then... shifting... I thought... maybe..."

Jiat chuffed. "Speak plainly, Ewan. You thought what?"

"Were you kissing her?"

"No." Jiat nuzzled my hot cheek. "I hugged her before she handed me the tray for breakfast. There is nothing between Hosanna and me but friendship."

Relief washed through me, and I felt foolish for a much different reason. "I'm sorry," I murmured.

"What we've done together has changed our

relationship, and I know you're uncertain." Jiat combed his fingers through my hair. "But when those uncertainties arise, come to me. Speak of them. Let me ease them for you."

I nodded. "I will." Since he'd invited me to share my worries, I decided then to voice them. "Hosanna said you could be charged because... because of me?"

Jiat pulled the tray up over our laps and poured hot tea into a cup for me. "Abomination is a charge one of our kind is leveled with when we take one of your kind as a lover. It's a serious charge, one that very few have escaped."

"And it would mean you'd die."

His hands paused as they spooned honey into my tea. After a moment, he nodded. "Yes. Those convicted go before the executioner's sword."

I licked my lips as I took my cup from him. "And the Human?"

"They disappear into the back room of the pound, and the body is incinerated afterward." Jiat looked at me. "But that isn't going to happen to either of us. Hyra and Jill manage to remain a secret, and so will we."

A lifetime of secrecy... but it was a lifetime with Jiat. I would happily accept that fate. I smiled at him. "It feels... different today. Everything seems brighter, louder."

Jiat chuckled. "Love. It has a habit of making everything shine."

I sipped my tea, the sweet, deep flavor warming me from the inside out. Spread out on the tray were all sorts of delights: fruit pastries, two plates of sliced meat, and a bowl of jewel-gold fruit. The smile I wore was so bright, it hurt my cheeks. "I love the golden fruits."

"I know." Jiat reached for the raw, red meat, his

favorite, and began to eat. I watched him, how the ruddy blood never stained his white-cream fur. He looked sideways at me after three mouthfuls. "Something else amiss?"

A blush warmed my face. "No. I just think you so beautiful. Not even the blood dares to mar you."

"Quite a poetic compliment. Thank you."

I dove into one of the fruit pastries, saving the gold-fruit for last. After the last bite of the fruit was in my belly, I sat back and stretched. "Is this what it will be like in the colony? The one you send other Humans to?"

"Freedom to love as our hearts desire? Yes. No fear of judgment or execution." Jiat purred and closed his eyes. "It's a place of equality and hard work, but well worth the sacrifices."

"What sacrifices?"

Jiat finished his meat and licked his fingers. "There aren't as many conveniences. I think they're still building their irrigation and working on plumbing, but I believe this is the sixth year with a positive crop, and they've finally sorted out their livestock. It's very simple. The houses aren't grand, or even as nice as the lower city homes. Huts. Log homes. I know they plan to eventually create more permanent, sturdy housing. Practical, but better. In the end, it's freedom versus oppression."

I let that linger between us for a bit, chewing over his words. The way Jiat said 'oppression' pulled at my thoughts. "Why haven't you gone to the colony yet? If... if the oppression bothers you..."

Jiat let out a slow breath. "I've thought I could do more here. As one of the Guard, I could intervene when possible. I have a spotless reputation, and so my adopting of pets is always thought of as noble. I give older pets good lives before their bodies give out. I was able to help the cause more in the city rather than in the colony."

"But now..."

"But now... I have you." Jiat's slitted, honey eyes turned back to me, pinned me with their sharp intelligence. "You mean more than the cause. I'd rather live out my life with you in the colony than remain here without you. Because, ultimately, you cannot remain with me in the city indefinitely. Suspicion will eventually arise. Love is so difficult to hide."

I furrowed my brow. "What about Hyra and Jill?"

Jiat shook his head. "Hyra plans to send Jill to the colony when the weather turns hot again, when it is safer for the long travel. They've been together too long, and I've noticed the sideways glances. Hyra loves Jill, but she doesn't want to risk Jill's life." He licked his lips and put the tray onto the side table. "Hyra will remain here in the city. It will break her heart. It will break Jill's. But, it's a necessary sacrifice to keep Jill alive."

"Will Hyra ever go to Jill?" My heart hurt for Jill! To lose Jiat would leave a gaping wound inside me. I couldn't imagine the pain Jill would endure.

"I don't know. That is a decision Hyra must make on her own and in her own time." Jiat pulled me into his arms. "It is something I am sure Hyra and Jill have spoken of many times."

I looked up at Jiat. "Would you send me away like that?"

"Of course not. We will remain in the city until I can sort through my affairs, and then we will go."

I couldn't help the smile that tugged at my lips. "It's

that simple?"

Jiat laughed and leaned down to lick sweetly across my lips. "No, Ewan, it isn't, but at the same time... it is."

The words made little sense, but I didn't care. All I wanted was to stay with Jiat, and I trusted him to keep us together. That little lick sent a tingle through my body, and a soft whimper made its way out of me. I pressed closer to Jiat, my hands hesitating a moment before reaching out to brush my fingers over his chest. His breath shivered out, his eyes fluttering for a moment, and I felt that surge of power within me again. It was intoxicating, and I hardened between my legs so quickly, it was almost painful.

After another lick from Jiat, another slow touch of my fingers to his nipples, he rolled us over so that he blanketed my body with his own. It was a heady sensation. Jiat was so broad, muscled under my shaking hands. The thick heat of him—damp with his desire for me—rubbed against me, alongside my cock. My head spun as we kissed, rocked into each other. Our panted breaths filled the air, and though I would have welcomed him inside my body all over again, Jiat never asked. The simple rocking, the breathless kisses and teasing touches, were all he wanted. All I needed. Time stopped for us, and our world narrowed to each other. I'd never felt something so intense, something I knew was as fleeting as it was lasting. I was more than a pet; he was more than a master. Together, we were so much more, and I wanted to hang onto it with both hands.

I gasped against his furry muzzle as the pleasure took me and I shook beneath him. All I saw were amber eyes dark with passion for me. For *me*. Jiat growled, his clawed hands tightening on my body, and then I felt the wet rush of his release across my skin. Our fluids mixed against my belly, and I sagged, a silly smile on my lips as I moaned. It was like a brand on my soul, and the mingled scent of our musk was my new favorite smell. I wanted to roll in it.

Jiat nuzzled my temple and chuffed softly. "A bath is now in order," he rumbled.

I laughed, happy and drunk with the afterglow. "But I like smelling of you."

Jiat purred at that and held me a little tighter. I closed my eyes, my belly full and my passion spent, and was content to just doze with him as the sunlight moved across the room.

Chapter Nine

Every year, the city lit up with the Spring Festival. Streets were crammed with stalls selling clothing, shoes, art, food. Jiat took me into one of the crowded streets, his collar warm on my throat and his leash leading me through the throng safely. My feet were clad in new sandals, and I had been recently groomed by Kosi. I thought everyone had to know how Jiat and I lived, loved, as if it were a mark on my very flesh, but no one gave us a second look. I didn't feel safe, but I also wasn't afraid. As long as I continued to behave as I had before all things changed, no one would be the wiser. I kept my eyes downcast and my feet three steps behind Jiat.

So much life around us! Myriad voices echoed in my ears, and I stole glimpses here and there. The sun was bright, the breeze cool, and the colors and scents from each stall beckoned me. Jiat stopped at several of the stalls, buying bits of art, a new loincloth, and six books. I carried what I could, but by midday, my stomach ached with hunger. I didn't want to be too forward as I stood there, Jiat talking with one of the beautiful, caramel colored cats outside the sweets stall. She didn't look to be of noble birth or pure bloodline, and Jiat laughed when she spoke of her betrothed's drunken antics the previous night. I wondered about their marriage customs. I'd never been kept long enough—or by someone unattached—to even know how the Felines and Canines married and bred. I chewed on that, lost in my own thoughts, until a gentle tug at my leash brought me back to the present. The female had disappeared into the stall, and Jiat was grinning at me.

"Daydreaming?" he asked.

I shook my head. "There's so much to look at!" I couldn't help but smile back at him. "And... and my stomach is very empty."

Jiat nodded. "It's well after noon. I know a perfect food stall that sells pastries filled with savory meats." My eyes must have lit up because Jiat laughed and began to lead me through the crowd once more. "Pastries and perhaps some dandelion wine, and then we will return home."

"My mouth is watering already," I said, a slight, excited hop to my steps. When we neared the stall, there was a short line. Jiat took me to a small part of grass between two stalls, attaching my leash to one of the stakes set there for just that purpose.

"I won't be long," Jiat promised. "You can sit, if you like. The grass is cool and soft. I'll bring the food back, and we can eat it as we begin home."

I watched him go to the stall and step in line. As long as I could see him, I didn't worry. Maybe, if this had been within the first few weeks with Jiat, I would have panicked. But not now. Now, I closed my eyes and turned my face up to the sun. Sitting on the cool grass was an inviting proposition, but Jiat had said he'd be quick. And I'd just been groomed, too. No, I'd stand and wait.

"Well, look at this hairless mutt!"

The voice was sharp, and there was something

under it that I didn't like. I didn't look for who had said it. That would have been above my place. I kept my eyes closed, my face upturned. If I ignored him, maybe he'd just go away.

"Look at him?" Someone snorted nearby. "Hell, I can *smell* him from here."

I finally opened my eyes and glanced around. There were three of the Guard standing ten paces away, leering at me. Another Jaguar like Jiat, but not unique in color. There was one of the Lynx bloodline, and the third was a slim, wiry-looking Fox with a rusty coat. I swallowed against the dryness of my throat and tried not to make eye contact with any of them. These were Jiat's fellow Guardsmen, and the last thing I wanted was to draw attention to us.

"I dunno," the Jaguar said, and I could feel his eyes crawl over my skin. "He's adorable, I suppose, except for those big, dumb cow eyes."

Oh, my cheeks burned, but I hoped they thought it merely from the sun. These were the ones who wanted to keep us as pets. Keep us on our hands and knees, eating table scraps and beaten when we didn't behave. These three embodied everything Jiat wanted so desperately to change, and I felt a fire in the pit of my belly that hungered for that very change.

The Fox snorted. "I know! It's why I could never own one. They're just so *stupid*," he sneered.

The Jaguar spoke up again. "I've read that some of them can speak as well as we do."

"They just mimic us." The Lynx was the one who had started the whole discussion about me. There was a cruel, cold edge to his voice that grated at me. "They can't possibly understand the words." When he spoke next, it was directly to me, his tone mocking, silly and nasty. "Who's a dumb cow? That's right! You are! You're a brainless little fuck, aren't you? Yes, you are!"

My cheeks *burned*, and my eyes darted around trying to find Jiat. I couldn't see him; the crowd had grown as the men taunted me. I fidgeted with my leash, fear making my heart race. What if they attacked me? Would anyone here stop them?

"Oh, leave him alone, Kayn," the Jaguar sighed.

"Lighten up; it's not like it can understand me," Kayn said with a shrug.

"That's almost worse," the Jaguar said with a shake of his head. "It's like making fun of the crippled. It's not his fault he's a stupid mongrel. Look at that blush, and his eyes shine with tears. You've made him sad!"

Bringing attention to my humiliation only made it worse. I didn't want to cry. I swallowed it down and looked away from them. I wouldn't give them the satisfaction of seeing me weep. These were the men who protected the city? They were cowards, picking on someone who couldn't fight back.

The Fox laughed. "Don't worry. He'll forget all about it in a few minutes. They only have a tiny memory, anyway."

"Exactly," Kayn said, his muzzle split in amusement. "It's too stupid to realize how stupid it is, so what difference does it make?"

"The difference," Jiat snarled, "is that *this* 'hairless mutt' belongs to a superior officer, and he expects you to show due deference and respect to his possessions!" Jiat towered above the three Guards, his eyes blazing like the sun and his shoulders tense. His tail shivered, and everything about him warned that all should tread carefully. My relief at having him at my side once more was palpable.

All three stood to attention, and Kayn quickly said, "Sir!"

Jiat's tail waved in great arcs. "This is *my* pet, and he is hardly stupid. And while you may believe he has a tiny memory, I do not. Report to my office tomorrow at dawn, is that understood?"

"Yes, sir!" they all said in unison, and then quickly dispersed. I could hear them grumble to each other, but not what they said. From the way Jiat's ears twitched, he did, and by the stars, what I would have given to be in that office at dawn!

I licked my lips and whispered, "I'm sorry."

Jiat's eyes focused on me, and none of the tension left him. "You've no reason to be sorry." He untied my leash, our lunch in a bag he carried, but I didn't think either of us was in the mood for food at that moment. "Come on. Let's go to the lake to eat. It's less crowded there. Quieter."

I nodded, but I don't think Jiat even noticed. I followed him, head bowed, and the bright afternoon seemed darkened even without a single cloud in the sky.

After supper, as I sat in Jiat's study and read one of the books Jiat had bought me at the Spring Festival that day, Jiat came and sat beside me. He waited a moment, and then eased the book from my hand.

"I will need to leave the house tomorrow before first light."

I nodded. "To meet with those three Guardsmen."

Jiat sighed, saving my place in the book with a ribbon. "Ewan, you do understand our position, right?"

I furrowed my brow. Our position? "We're not supposed to be lovers."

"Yes, and that means we must continue to behave as we ever have. I know we had the majority of winter away from prying eyes." Snow made it difficult for pets to go out unless properly clothed, and I didn't own many outfits fit for the cold. I didn't mind because it meant I'd spent much of my time with Jiat, tangled in our bedsheets. "But with spring and summer, we will be outside more. Attending events. Visiting people. I will take you with me as I shop for food and supplies. There is a way we must continue to behave so we do not draw suspicion our way."

"But, I didn't behave any differently today than I ever have," I whispered. Had I done it wrong? I shifted on the divan. "I'm sorry if I let on somehow. I tried—"

"It wasn't you," Jiat murmured, the tip of his tail slowly tapping against my thigh. "It was me. I overreacted with those Guardsmen, and I will have to try to control the damage when they present themselves to me in the morning. But, I know Kayn. He isn't one to forget a slight, and we had many eyes on us this afternoon when I dressed them down. If he can knock me down, I know he will. I have to be more careful." He smiled and cupped my cheek. "I have to not love you so much when we're in the public eye."

I leaned into the palm of his hand for a moment, and then I moved across the divan and into Jiat's lap. "I understand." I stroked my fingers through his fur, and then leaned in to nuzzle his throat. "But when we're not in the public eye..."

Jiat chuckled, and the tension that had plagued him since the confrontation seemed to drain from him. His hands smoothed up and down my back, pulling me closer. "When we're not in the public eye, I can love you as much as I like."

That flutter of desire uncoiled in my belly as we pressed close together on the divan. "And how much would you like to love me now?"

"Until we are sweaty, spent, and sated," Jiat growled, lifting me and carrying me from the study.

My heart raced as need pooled between my legs, and I welcomed his hands and tongue on my body, aching to have him inside me once more. I wanted to feel everything with him, to hear his growls and purr, to feel his seed coat me inside and out as I cried out his name. Under the surging of his body, I forgot about the Guardsmen and the humiliation and fear. Chasing away the shadows, Jiat loved me well into the night, until we were as he'd wanted: sweaty, spent, and sated.

Chapter Ten

For nearly two weeks, we walked on eggshells, tense and waiting. Jiat had tried to lessen the blow he'd given the Guardsmen's pride, but I knew he didn't believe he'd done enough. We didn't venture out much, and when we did, it exhausted me. I second guessed everything I did, every look, every breath. Even if it was merely an outing to collect fresh meat and greens, by the time we returned, I was shaking and near tears. It felt as if eyes were always on us now, whispered words in the shadows threatening what I'd only just gained. As the one year anniversary of my adoption loomed, we began to let ourselves relax. Jiat didn't keep the leash as tight, and I didn't keep my eyes trained to the ground whenever we left the house.

I don't know what tipped them off. I don't know if they really needed an excuse, or if they just came for me. Hosanna was at the market while Jiat was at the Guard House, and I was told to stay inside. I was not to answer the door, and it never occurred to me to break that rule. I was reading near a side window when the knock came. I ignored it. This was not *my* house, and Jiat had left me with clear orders to never open the door. I wasn't about to break the rule now.

The second knock was louder, harder. I frowned

and turned the page. Hosanna would be home soon, and if the person was intent on leaving a message for Jiat, they could wait outside for her.

There was no third knock. Instead, the door burst open, thrown off its hinges, and three men I'd never seen before walked inside. I couldn't help but shake, terror seizing me. They were Felines, but that was all I noticed as the biggest one came at me, growling as his large, clawed hand wrapped around my arm. I cried out as he yanked me out of the house.

"Stop!" I shouted and thrashed, panic squeezing my heart. "What are you doing! Where are we going! Where is my master!" I wanted Jiat. Jiat would stop them, would make them let me *go*.

The Feline bruising my arm stopped us in the middle of the street. "Your master has been arrested. Abomination."

That word. The world fell away with that one word as I stared up at the cat with fear in my eyes. I was being taken from Jiat. Whatever had happened... whatever look or thought had betrayed us... I was being taken away. "I want my master," I whispered brokenly.

"You have no master any more," one of the other Felines hissed. "To the pound you go, mongrel, and there you'll be destroyed."

They yanked me along, and I thought I was going to throw up. No trial. No reprieve. Just a death sentence. Numbly, I asked, "And what of my master?"

"That is for the magistrate to decide." The smallest Feline glanced back at me after speaking, and I thought I saw a spark of pity in his eyes, but it was gone as soon as I blinked.

Human Rights

By the time we arrived at the pound, my feet were blistered and bloody, and I'd thrown up twice. I ached to see Jiat, to take comfort in him, but he was nowhere. I didn't know if they were holding him or if he had washed his hands of me to save himself. I wouldn't have blamed him. I came face to face with Miab, and I whimpered, recoiling.

"I knew you would be back here," Miab said. "I just didn't realize what filth you really were." He wrapped one of the pound's collars around my throat and clipped a leash to it.

The Guards left me with him, and I almost pleaded with them to stay with me. Miab drew his cane up and brought it down on the back of my thighs. The pain was so intense, so sudden, that I pitched forward and slammed my knees into the hard, unforgiving floor. My scream echoed in the receiving room, and it died out into sobs. I'd never felt such hopelessness as I did then, my thighs burning, my feet in agony, and the thickness of my anguish threatening to suffocate me.

Miab yanked on the leash. "Crawl, mutt."

I tried to crawl, but Miab mostly dragged me behind him. I didn't go into the exam room. I wasn't taken into a waiting cage to be put into the general pound. No, I was led to The Door. The door no pet wanted to go through. Behind that door, there was a bank of half a dozen cages, and only one had anyone in it. Miab opened the one next to the other pretty female pet and shoved me in, slamming and locking the door behind me. He crouched down, his nasty face pressed to the bars.

"Just waiting for the magistrate's signature, and then we'll put you out of your misery."

When he left, I actually felt relief.

And then I wept.

I don't know how long I wept, but when I quieted, the female next to me sniffled. She peered at me through the crisscrossing bars, her blue eyes red and tired. "What did you do?" she whispered.

I shook my head, a sob threatening as I breathed, "I loved my master."

No other explanation was needed. She bit her lip and shook her head. "I... I've been told by Dr. Tiwan that it doesn't hurt."

"I want my master." I just wanted Jiat. If I had to die, I wanted Jiat at my side.

I was almost finally, blissfully, asleep when the lights flickered on, too bright and painful. I squinted and tried to shy away. Two of the Guard stopped in front of my cage, and Miab was glowering beside them. It looked like they had woken him. His fur and clothing were wrinkled. I blinked several times, pressed to the very back of my cage. One of the Guardsman—a Jaguar—nodded in my direction.

"Open it."

Miab huffed, but he didn't argue. He opened my cage and clipped a leash to my collar. I cried out as he yanked, forcing me from the cage and onto the cold tile. I thought he would keep hold of the leash, but he passed it to the canine Guardsman.

"There are four rooms—"

The Jaguar shot him a bland look. "We will not interrogate him here," he spat, and I could hear the disdain in his voice. "I will send word when it's time for you to fetch him."

Miab glared, his tail shivering. "Fetch him?"

Human Rights

The Canine—Jackal or Coyote?—yanked on my leash. "The warden told you to cooperate, Miab. Word will be sent when you're needed."

I crawled after the Guardsmen as we left Miab and the pound behind. My knees ached as they led me through the city. I didn't dare look up, speak, and if I could have not breathed, I would have stopped in an instant. Anything to keep them from paying any sort of close attention to me. Attention could mean pain from Guardsmen like these. Jiat had told me once that there were others in his ranks at the Guard who believed as he did. Had the Guard found them all out? Were they all on trial now? Or was it just Jiat and me? My chin trembled, and my eyes stung. Jiat. What was happening to him?

The Guardsmen pulled me along until my knees throbbed from the cobbled road. I wanted to stop them, to hold my knees close, but I couldn't. I was sure if I stopped or balked, they'd just drag me behind them. I bit into my lower lip. I was panting, and there was a minute tremor moving through me by the time they stopped at a set of white, intricately carved doors. I swooned on my hands and knees, worried I might vomit. The doors opened, and we left the city behind, the cobbled road turning into smooth, cool tile under my protesting knees. It was a small blessing, one I didn't take for granted.

By the time they shoved me into a tiny, dimly lit room with no windows, I was parched, dizzy, and exhausted. And I had the return trip to look forward to because Miab certainly wasn't going to rent a cart to take me back. I leaned back into the farthest corner of the room and drew my knees up. They were torn. Bloody. I bowed my head and allowed myself a small bout of weeping.

113

Everything hurt. My stomach gnawed at me. The thirst was terrible. I wanted cool water, warm food, and Jiat's big, gentle hands on my body. I didn't bother to look up when the door opened and then shut. If it wasn't Jiat, I didn't care.

"They tell me your name is Ewan; is that right?" It was a female voice, soft and tender. I looked up in surprise. The visitor was one of the Cheetahs, tall and sleek, draped in the robes of a magistrate. She took in my disheveled state and hissed in the back of her throat. I cowered deeper into the corner, but her anger wasn't directed at me. "I'm going to make sure someone comes and takes a look at those knees. But would it be all right if we talked for a little while first?"

I licked my lips and swallowed against a dry throat. "All right." I didn't trust any of them, really, but my knees *hurt*.

She smiled at me, her teeth sharp in her muzzle. "Good." She walked to the door and spoke softly to someone outside, and then shut the door once more. "Water will come shortly, as will a physician. While we wait, I'd like you to tell me about your master."

"Tell you about Sir Jiat?" I frowned. "He's... my master."

"Yes," she said with a slight nod. "Do you love your master?"

I felt a chasm open up before me. A maze to navigate. "Yes," I said slowly. "He is the kindest master I have ever had."

"Sir Jiat is a decorated member of the Guard. He has served the Court for many years without fail." She sat down in the only chair in the room and smoothed her robes. "Recently, though, it has come to our attention that he might be associated with the wrong sorts of people."

"Wrong sorts?" My stomach dropped. I knew what she was after now. She was after the Movement. Jiat and the network that helped to save the Humans. "T-There are wrong sorts?"

Again, she smiled at me, but this time, I could see it didn't really reach her eyes. "Yes, Ewan. The kind that think in a radically different way. The kind that believe anarchy and disorder are the answer to social ills they themselves have created."

"I... I don't understand."

The door opened, and a young Jackal stepped in with a glass of water and a small kit. "There are injuries?"

"Yes," she said, motioning to me. "It seems the road was difficult for Ewan's knees. Please tend them. The water is for him, too."

The physician knelt in front of me and offered the glass. I glanced between them before taking the glass and sipping the water. I turned most of my attention back to the Cheetah, ignoring the Jackal as he began to clean and dress my knees. "I don't understand," I said once more, my voice stronger after the water.

"There is an order to our city. You Humans, who have no means of protecting yourselves or contributing to our society, are kept in comfort, your basic needs met. You are not treated badly, are you?" she asked.

I hissed as the Jackal smeared salve over my knees. "N-No," I whispered. It was a lie, though. Humans were treated worse than the cities horses and work animals. We could be beaten, kept outside, thrown away! We had no *dignity*, which was a word Jiat had taught me. In this city, Humans possessed no dignity, and Jiat and his *radical thinking* only said we should.

She smiled at me again. She smiled too much. "No." The Jackal stood up, nodded to her, and slipped back out of the room. "Tell me, Ewan, did Sir Jiat ever take you to gatherings?"

"I was taken to play with other pets." There was nothing wrong with that, I knew. "Other pets came to Sir Jiat's home to play with me."

"That... was so kind of him. Did he ever speak to the masters of those other pets?"

"Yes." I forced a smile to my lips. "They would have lunch while we played out in the courtyard."

My smile seemed to please her, and she leaned forward. "Did you ever hear what they said?"

I would not betray Jiat. This female was insane if she thought I'd just hand over all of Jiat's secrets to her. "Sometimes. They would talk about a loss of life or current court matters or debate over the expansion of livestock lands." I forced myself to look away, as if embarrassed. "I didn't understand it most of the time."

She nodded. Everyone "knew" that Humans didn't have the same mental capacities of the Canines and Felines. We were just dumb, hairless creatures, after all. It occurred to me that keeping her believing that was in my best interests for now.

"Did they ever talk about anything else?" she prodded. "Maybe traveling to another city, or about pets that went away on a long trip?"

I almost laughed in her face. She was so transparent. She was asking about the colony, as though I would be stupid enough to just blurt out everything. I shook my head, letting my eyes go as wide and stupid as I could manage. "I never heard anything like that."

"No one would be mad at you if you did. You're not in trouble, Ewan. You understand that, right?"

Of course I was in trouble. If they took Jiat away from me, there was only one place that I could go, and then only one place after that. "I understand." Better than she thought.

"So think hard. Can you remember anything else about those other masters? Could you maybe point at them if I showed you some pictures?"

"I don't think so. Everyone looks so different in pictures than they do from the ground."

Something in the way I said that made her whiskers twitch, and I instantly regretted it. She looked back at the door for a moment and made sure it was secure, and then she walked across the room and crouched down in front of me.

"We both know you're not as stupid as you're pretending to be." Her voice was still soft, but the gentleness had been replaced with steel. "Your master and his friends are in a lot of trouble. They are dangerous, and they need to be stopped. We've made an offer to him that if he tells us about the others in his little revolution, the Court will be lenient in his sentencing. But he refuses to help himself, so I'm making the same offer to you. Tell me what you know about this so-called Movement, and I can make sure that both you and he are treated fairly. You won't be allowed to be back together, of course, but we will find you a new home with a new master who will care for you properly. I think you already know what the alternative is."

I stared back at her, too stunned at the change in tone to respond immediately. Outside of Jiat and the other masters like him, I'd never heard anyone admit that Humans were smart enough to understand things on the same level as the Canines and Felines. How many people felt the same way, but couldn't take the next step and admit that we should be treated on the same level?

I licked my lips and held her gaze, all pretending gone. Very slowly, deliberately, I said, "I don't know anything. I really can't help you."

I braced myself for the inevitable attack, the shouting or the beating, but the Cheetah simply sighed and stood, smoothing down her robes with her paws. "No, I suppose you really can't," she said, just like that switching back to the kindly voice from before, though this one seemed to be tinged with a note of sadness. She walked back to the door, but before opening it, she looked back over her shoulder at me. When she spoke, her voice was barely above a whisper. "For what it's worth, I wish you luck."

And then she was gone. Miab appeared some time later and walked me back to the pound, the Cheetah's parting words still pounding in my ears.

I don't know how long I was left in the cage at the pound. I lost my company when Dr. Tiwan took the female from the cage beside my own a day after I was interrogated. Miab dropped food and water into my cage a few times, though I never ate. I didn't want anything but Jiat. I slept a lot, and since there were no windows, the passage of time was difficult to note. When I'd finally given up on Jiat coming for me, he appeared in the doorway. I sat up, gripping the lattice metal of my cage, and gave a cry. He hurried to me and crouched down, brushing his fingers over mine through the metal.

"Shh," Jiat breathed. "I'm so sorry. This is all my doing—"

"Take me home," I begged, tears in my eyes again. "Please... please, Jiat, take me *home*."

Jiat shook his head, his own eyes shining with tears. "I can't. Oh, Ewan, I can't. The magistrate signed the order today. I've been expelled from the Guard, and... and no one will speak to me. No one *can* speak to me. I've been given a ten year sentence, ostracized by all in the city."

I bowed my head and cried all over again, bitterness a hard lump in my throat. "Please..."

"I wish I could," Jiat said, his voice choked, uneven. "Miab is watching us now. I asked to see you through to the end, but I was only granted five minutes."

Five minutes! Only five? I surged forward, pressing my lips to the metal. "I love you."

Jiat pressed his muzzle to my lips, lapped at my tear-wet skin. "I love you, too. That has not changed. It will not change."

His scent filled my nose, and I could feel the softness of his fur. I wanted to be held by him, protected, but I knew this was it. This was all I would have before my end came for me. My tears fell unchecked, and I kept whispering my love to him, even after Miab yanked Jiat from me, leaving me alone in the room.

Chapter Eleven

Thirty-two years. My life had lasted but thirty-two years. Maybe I'd expected longer, even if I really had no reason to. Mutts didn't last long. But once I'd entered Jiat's home, I'd thought to live until I was old, my body creaky, safe and warm and loved. This *society*, though... Humans so far down, animals and slaves, even with masters and mistresses who loved us. Love didn't change the way the laws bound everyone. I just hoped Jill would escape. Even if she had to leave Hyra—no matter the heartbreak of that parting—at least Jill would be alive. Hyra would know they always had the *chance* to reunite. Jiat didn't have that chance. Our chance was gone.

The hunger had long stopped bothering me, but the thirst was nearly unbearable. I eyed the bowl of water. Would it matter if I died of whatever awaited me or from denying myself water? I swallowed again, but it hurt. My tongue felt thick in my mouth, and my throat burned like the summer sun. The water called to me, and I squeezed my eyes shut. No! I wouldn't.

But the more I thought about it, the more my mind came back to the same conclusion: this was my own punishment. I suppose I felt guilty wanting even the basic necessities when I couldn't be sure what Jiat's sentence would ultimately mean for him. That aside, it was nothing more than pride, and even that was failing me now. I sighed, a rasping sound, and then weakly crawled to the water bowl. I finished it in three huge gulps, and I wanted more. I wouldn't beg for it. I wouldn't ask. Miab would bring more eventually, probably with a smug smile on his lips to see my bowl empty finally.

I sat back in the corner and closed my eyes. How long would I wait? If my life was to end, I wanted it to be done with. I was ready. No, no, I wasn't. I didn't *want* to die. I wanted to go home. I wanted to curl up in Jiat's arms and weep with relief and joy. Instead, tears of grief stung my swollen sinuses. I couldn't smell Jiat on me anymore. How long had it been since he'd whispered his goodbyes to me? A day? A week? I hugged myself and hid my face in my knees. I was so tired, so lost, and there was no reprieve. No one was going to save me. I was done.

"Ewan?"

I looked up, blinking blearily. Had I fallen asleep? Dr. Tiwan crouched in front of my cage, watching me. I didn't speak. There was no point in speaking. The beasts that lorded over this place wouldn't hear my words, anyway. I was an animal, sent to be deposed of by a court that probably didn't even know my name. No one knew my name. Ewan. Ha! The name my first owner had given me, but not the one my own mother had whispered into my ear as a child. My name. I would keep it for myself. I would go to my grave with it in my heart.

"Ewan."

That name. A name I'd come to for so many years, but a name that wasn't my own. Let him call me that name until time stopped. It wasn't my name. I bowed my head. If he'd come to strip me of my life, let him get on with it. No begging, no weeping, no struggling. I wouldn't give them that. I would keep those pieces for myself. They couldn't have those, just like they couldn't have my love of Jiat. I would go into that darkness loving Jiat, and that was mine, too. My love and my name, mine. The only two things I'd *ever* owned in my life.

The cage door swung open, screeching loudly on its hinges. Dr. Tiwan clipped a leash to the rough, ill-fitting collar around my neck. A tug and I crawled out. I kept my head bowed as Dr. Tiwan led me away from the bank of cages and to a door at the back of the room. The room. That place all pets whispered about in the pound. No pet who walked through the door stepped back out. It was the end. My end. I'd be lying if I denied the fear that rushed through me, the fluttering of my heart and the tightening of my gut. I wanted to run. I wanted to beg. But I gritted my teeth and swallowed it all down. I wouldn't give them *that.*

The room was small. I jumped a little as the door shut behind me with a soft click. Dr. Tiwan threw the bolt, and I stared at the metal table surrounded by little else. A single cabinet stood in the corner, a drab gray-green monolith in the stark room. Beside the table was a tray with a vial of pale green liquid and a syringe. I stared at it, tilting my head. That was it? That was what would take me from this life? It seemed so small for such a thing.

"Please," Dr. Tiwan murmured. "Lay on the table. I would rather not call Miab in and make this... any more difficult for you than I know it must be."

My gaze moved from the tray to Dr. Tiwan, my brow furrowed. "Difficult?" I asked, my voice rough. "You think this difficult?"

"I know it is." Dr. Tiwan went to the small, basic sink to our left and washed his hands. "Death is never easy."

"Of course it is." I glanced to the tray. "For you, it's as simple as a green liquid and a needle."

Dr. Tiwan turned as he dried his hands. "The taking of a life—*any* life—is difficult for a physician. I assure you, though, it is quiet. Like falling asleep. Painless."

I stared at the metal table, listening to my own heart beat in my chest. It wasn't racing anymore. If there was fear, I didn't feel it. Painless. Like falling asleep. How merciful. Useless mercy, I thought, since that mercy still denied me my life. It still left Jiat alone, cast out from his own life, for ten years. I crossed to the table and crawled up on it, hissing at the chill. It brought gooseflesh up all over my body. Staring up at the ceiling, I waited.

"Close your eyes."

"No."

"Ewan." Dr. Tiwan stood over me, his furry face compassionate. "Close your eyes."

I met his gaze. "No." I wouldn't make it any easier for him. This was *my* death, not his.

Dr. Tiwan sighed, and I watched him draw some of the pale green liquid up into the syringe. I suddenly wanted to close my eyes. I righted my head and let my eyes shut. Jiat. I conjured a picture of my master. Fur white with those tan, beautiful markings. Eyes the color of deep amber honey. His voice. That slight growl when I touched him, and the deep purring when our passions were spent. I tried to keep myself there, in that warm memory, even when I felt the sting of the needle pierce the flesh of my arm. The liquid burned, and within moments, my head began to swim.

Human Rights

The vision of Jiat blurred, like looking at the landscape through a rainy window. Everything became so warm, and my thoughts slowed. Sound disappeared, but I clung to the memory of that purr even as darkness rushed up to swallow me whole.

The last thought I remembered having was that Dr. Tiwan was wrong. The pain of losing the memory of Jiat's purr was the worst of my life, and then there was nothing.

Chapter Twelve

My head was pounding. It reminded me of when I'd turned nineteen and was given glass after glass of the spiked punch. I'd woken with a headache much like this one. I moaned and brought my hand up to my head.

Wait.

Hand. Head. There was no silence, no darkness. I was thirsty. How could I be dead *and* thirsty?

I tried to sit up, force my eyes to open, but a broad hand pressed me back down. Finally, my eyes cooperated, and my vision filled with the sight of Jiat hovering worriedly over me. Jiat! But, oh, my head!

"Shh," Jiat purred. "You've been asleep for almost two days." He lifted a cup and brought it to my lips. It tasted of water and something sweet, a little sour. I watched him unblinkingly as I slowly sipped. "I am so sorry," he whispered, nuzzling my temple. "I wanted to tell you Tiwan was one of us. Whenever a pet is to be destroyed for anything other than murder, Tiwan puts them into a deep sleep, and we smuggle them to the colony. We didn't tell you in case Miab witnessed your execution." Jiat's whiskers twitched. "Miab is a pain in the ass, and is most certainly not part of the Movement."

After finishing the cup of liquid, I licked my dry

lips. It took three tries to make my tongue and throat work, for me to ask the one question burning in my mind. "I'm alive?"

Jiat set the cup aside and drew me into his arms. "Yes."

Tears gathered in my eyes as I reached up to brush my fingers over Jiat's face. "I'm alive!" I gasped. I rose up enough to kiss all over Jiat's muzzle, holding tightly to him, my fingers tangling in his fur. "And you're here... with me."

"My life in the city meant nothing if I could not share it with you. I told you as much," Jiat said, his hands smoothing over my bare skin. "I love you."

I laughed as my tears fell. "We're here... in the colony?"

Jiat chuffed. "In the colony, and in our simple, new home."

"And Hosanna?"

"Hosanna has gone to live and work for Hyra. Together, they will continue where I no longer can." Jiat licked at my throat and cheek, taking the tears from my skin. "This is our life now. Equality and nothing to hide." He grinned at me. "Would you like to see your new home?"

See the colony. It was frightening and exciting, and I nodded. "Please." I wanted to walk, to breathe in fresh air.

Jiat helped me up, and I looked around our home. It was simple. Clay brick walls with mud between the bricks. The roof was a tight thatch. It was one room, but with windows on each side. Simple screens were stretched over the windows. A table and four chairs, a divan, a crude kitchen, and the bed I'd been in with Jiat. I chewed at my lip. "This is so unlike your grand home."

"I like it. It has... potential." Jiat held out a dark blue

cloth. "I will build bookshelves, a desk. We will improve our kitchen. We will make our life here, Ewan. Nothing handed to us, everything earned. Together."

I stared at the cloth in Jiat's hand. "What's that?"

Jiat chuffed. "Your loincloth. We will have more clothing made for you in time, but for now, this will have to do."

I took the loincloth from Jiat, my throat tight. Clothing. My own *clothing*. Jiat helped me to tie the loincloth, and I knew then I'd been elevated. I'd gained something I'd never dreamed of having: freedom. Jiat took my hand and tugged me through our front door and outside. It was bright, hot. Summer had come? I looked up at Jiat, his coat practically glowing in the sunlight.

"How long...?"

Jiat squeezed my hand. "Mid-spring when you went into the pound. It is now the first month of summer."

I looked around. Other similar homes were near our own, many with their doors and windows thrown open to the afternoon heat. Every home had a small garden, vegetables climbing trellises and reaching toward the bright blue sky. I turned back to our home and, yes, we also had a patch of land cultivated and ready to grow things. I smiled, hope bubbling up inside me.

"Ewan!"

I spun around in time to see Jill rushing up to me, smiling, her body covered by a simple dress that stopped mid-thigh. "Jill?"

"I'd heard you'd been brought here, that Jiat had arrived." She hugged me and kissed my cheek. "I'm so glad you're all right. Hrya was so worried about you."

I blinked. "Hyra is here?"

A look of pain streaked across Jill's face before she smiled at me again. "No. She's needed in the city. I... I understand that, even if it hurts. She'll come to me, though, whenever she can. I'll wait."

Her devotion made me smile. I'd have waited for Jiat, too.

"I want to show Ewan around, Jill," Jiat said gently. "Come by after dark. Have supper with us. It won't be anything special, but—"

Jill grinned. "It'll be perfect, Jiat. I have to go help gather eggs, anyway. I'll bring some for you." She kissed my cheek again. "You'll love it here." Then she was gone, jogging down the dirt road and disappearing over the hill.

We walked all afternoon. No human was naked. There were no collars. No leashes. No one had their heads bowed or eyes averted. There was laughter. Sweat. Work. I saw humans paired off together, humans with canines or felines, felines and canines... there was no permutation I didn't see. Groups talking together. Playing games. And children! I saw *children* running around, chasing one another, humans and canines and felines. By the time we returned to our home, I was sun-flushed, heart racing, and mind whirling.

"It's perfect!" I cried once Jiat shut our door. "It's perfect, Jiat. Home is *here*. I want to be a part of it all. I want to make it work."

"It will take much work." Jiat went to a cupboard in our kitchen and returned with dried meats and fruit. "I have more of the juice I gave you earlier. You should eat. Rest for now."

I put the food on the table and threw my arms around him, kissing his muzzle. "I want to *celebrate*, Jiat, not rest!"

"And how would you like to celebrate, hmm?" Jiat asked, wrapping his arms around me and inching me back toward the bed.

"With pleasure and cries of passion and so much kissing, my lips ache from it," I declared.

Jiat and I tumbled back onto the bed, and his weight above me was one of the greatest pleasures, solid and real. "As you command, Ewan."

I smiled up at him, brushing my fingers near his eyes, honey eyes filled with love and warmth for me. He already had my love, and so I gave Jiat the only other thing I had kept for myself. "Westyn. My name is Westyn."

About the Author

    S.L. Armstrong has been writing for as long as she can remember. Art and reading have played a large part in her life since young childhood, but around fourteen, writing became her passion. Voraciously consuming every book in front of her opened up hundreds of worlds in her head, and she soon wanted to create worlds for other people as well. She has a particular fondness for gothic horror, horror, high fantasy, urban fantasy, and romance novels. The authors she turns to time and again are Stephen King, L.J. Smith, V.C. Andrews, R.L. Stine, and Anne Rice, among others. She has no shame in picking up the young adult novels she loved as a child, and she will talk your ear off about grammar and punctuation.

    After she married her husband sixteen years ago, she began to truly delve into the world of writing for public consumption. It was sheer chance that she stumbled on M/M fanfiction, and she's not looked back. Though fanfiction will always have a fond place in her heart, she soon grew tired of playing in other people's sandboxes. When she discovered M/M romance, and how it was now a legitimate branch of romance writing, she knew her course. S.L. plans to release F/F, M/M, M/F, and multiple partner books as she continues her writing career. M/M romance is where her heart lies, no matter what else she may write or read, and it's where she keeps returning to. There is something about two men passionately in love that just makes her heart melt, and she has no intention of giving that up any time soon.

S.L. Armstrong lives in Florida with her husband and her partner along with two dogs, and fifteen cats. She hates the heat and longs for a northern, snowy climate. She writes with K. Piet on a number of projects, but she also writes her own solitary titles as well. S.L. Armstrong owns Storm Moon Press LLC along with her husband and K. Piet.

S.L. Armstrong & K. Piet

Includes 12 black-and-white illustrations by Diana Callinger!

Zach is just seventeen years old, but despite his youth, he has more than his fair share of responsibility. An experimental fling in high school has led him down the path of single fatherhood. Now, he holds down a job, takes his college classes online, and pays his own bills as best he can—all while juggling daycare and chores and play-dates for his four-month-old, Mae. It's a rough, 24/7 life, but to Zach, Mae is worth every penny spent and every minute of his day.

With no free time to speak of, it feels like a miracle when Zach meets Wil in the check-out line at his work. Handsome, grounded, from the proverbial "right side of the tracks", and—even better—good with kids, Wil is everything he could want in a boyfriend. But as interested as Wil is in Zach, he has his own life, his own family, his own job and college career to think about. All the various draws on their time means that it's hard just to find chances to be together. But Zach's no stranger to hard tasks, and believes he owes it to himself to try.

Now available from Storm Moon Press!
Digital: $4.99/Print: $12.99

Other Side of Night
Bastian & Riley

S.L. Armstrong & K. Piet

Vampires walk among us. For centuries, they have adapted, learning to pass undetected in our world. They no longer fear the day, only the sting of direct sunlight. They are students, bankers, lawyers, and even actors. But when the sun goes down, they are all united by their eternal thirst. We do not see them from our safe and comfortable side of the night. But sometimes, one of us is drawn away from the light and we cross into their world. Into the other side of night.

Sebastian Rossi's second year at the University of Tennessee began much differently than his first. He rushes to and from his classes, covered head to toe in thick clothing. Parties are a thing of the past, and dating hasn't been high on his list of priorities. No, high on his needs is blood. Lots of it. Adjusting to the changes no one even told him would happen following one great night of partying and sex has been hell for Bastian, but he's managing.

Riley Lynch's dream is to be a veterinarian. He works hard to pay his tuition, reads in every spare moment, and tries to forget the nightmare of his sophomore year. Summer has washed away all the bad, leaving him refreshed and eager for his junior year at UT. Life is finally looking up for him, and he has no intention of sliding back down into the depression that had consumed him during his last relationship.

A chance meeting brings their two worlds into alignment and passion sparks between them. When Riley learns of the changes Bastian is going through, he has a choice to make: walk away or embrace the night.

Now available from Storm Moon Press!
Digital: $3.99/Print: $8.99

After a near-fatal accident, Logan Walker seeks help to control the compulsive blood fetish that almost cost his submissive's life. Help happens to be in the form of an athletic, smart psychologist by the name of Dr. Kasper Bromley. Kasper, though, soon finds himself swept up in the fantasies Logan came to him to control. Reluctantly throwing his ethics to the wind, Kasper submits himself to Logan, gambling his career, his future, and his heart on this intriguing man and the lifestyle he offers. But when Kasper's desires outpace Logan's, the young doctor is swept down into a whirlpool of sex and sadism that even Logan's love may not be enough to rescue him from.

Now available from Storm Moon Press!
Digital: $4.99/Print: $7.99